Mark … Hartlepool and
is no… and engineering
group… numerous articles and stories for
magazines and science fiction publications.

Also by Mark Adlard:

INTERFACE
VOLTEFACE

Mark Adlard

MULTIFACE

Futura Publications Limited
An Orbit Book

An Orbit Book

First published in Great Britain by
Sidgwick & Jackson Limited in 1975

First Futura Publications edition 1977

ISBN 0 8600 7971 6
Printed by
William Collins Sons & Co Ltd
London and Glasgow

Futura Publications Limited
110 Warner Road, Camberwell
London SE5

CHAPTER ONE

Will Forstell side-tracked into the slow lane in Thruway 2, and stepped on to the sidewalk as soon as he saw an empty space to put his feet.

He would soon be there!

This was the one time in the week when he truly lived. A contraction in his chest, a tightness in his stomach, told him that the excitement would always be there, no matter how many times the adventure were repeated. This was what life was really about.

He loathed his job as Chief Clerk in the Stock Control Department of Depot Number Five. He hated the stock list which he brought up to date each morning for the Planning Manager. He detested the advice notes, the receipt slips and the weight tickets, all of which provided the raw material on which he had to exercise his laborious arithmetic. He often thought it would do him good if, in some secret place, he could scream his execration of the whole damned system at intervals during each working day.

Will didn't suppose that the Planning Manager would mind very much, so long as he couldn't hear him. He rather liked the Planning Manager, although he called him 'Willy', and he was a good boss. Yet in some ways he was a mysterious man. He would take the new stock list each morning with a smile of thanks, and then proceed to scrutinize those columns of figures as if they held a message which he was for ever trying to decode.

They held nothing of the kind, Will thought savagely, as he continued along the sidewalk. There was one reason, and one reason only, for submitting to the tedium of working. And it didn't need any deciphering.

Anyone could live on the state annuity, and most people were content to do just that. That was fine if you wanted to rot away like a vegetable. But with the increments Will earned by working, he could afford to taste the special pleasures of the First Sector every week if he wanted to.

He did want to. And, by Christ, he was going to!

With eager steps he obeyed the directional signs, and turned into a side street. This week, at some extra charge, he was going to enjoy a preliminary and additional pleasure. He turned left in response to another sign, and began to walk in a direction parallel to Thruway 2.

The new facility was ahead of him. Suspended in the air, huge electroluminous letters glowed :

AUTOTERMINUS – SECOND SECTOR.

Will found that his steps had begun to falter. He discovered a tiny seed of misgiving, which must have been lodged inside him since he left the Fifth Sector, but which he'd refused to acknowledge. His apprehension grew as those giant letters began to tower above him.

Perhaps he was a coward. Perhaps he shouldn't go on. Perhaps it would be stupid for him to try, even if it wasn't stupid for other people.

There was still time to change his mind and go the way he'd always gone before. All he had to do was retrace his steps to Thruway 2, return to the centre, go round a short segment of the ringline, and exit on to the southbound paveline in Thruway 1. He could forget about the new facility.

Will Forstell suddenly ached to do things the way he'd done them before. He wanted the old familiar ways.

It was curious that he should think of any route through Tcity as being familiar. How could anything be familiar when all routes looked exactly the same?

The thruways radiated from the central core with the predictable symmetry of spokes in a wheel, and they were fed and drained by the two-way pavelines which shuffled their human cargoes between the ringline and the city walls. Alongside the thruways ran the beeblocks, stahlex honeycombs, reproducing themselves in an endless progression as far as the eye could see. Each beeblock faced its mirror image on the other side of the thruways, like miners' houses of the olden days in the Welsh valleys or on the Northumbrian coast, but swollen to unimaginable size. They were so high that they seemed to lean towards each other and almost touch each other's foreheads.

Nevertheless, for Will Forstell, the route between those identical blocks had taken on something which might be called familiarity. In any case the uniform façades of the First Sector were broken up to some extent by buildings which had been particularized in some way. As you travelled south in Thruway 1 you saw the big dome of the Fun Palace on your left, and after a few hundred metres you passed the triangular doorway of the Blue Star Club on your right.

He had paid his maiden visit to the First Sector after receiving his first increment for working at Depot Number Five, and since then he'd made the trip every week. He made the journey to the pleasure grounds of the First Sector with something akin to the blind instinct by which swallows and salmon return to their well-loved nests and spawning grounds.

To hell with it! Hundreds of people – no, thousands, perhaps hundreds of thousands – had started to travel this way as a matter of routine. If they could do it, why shouldn't he? He *wasn't* stupid.

Will approached the barrier and jostled his way into one of the queues. When his turn came he placed his credit card in the slot, held it there until there was a click, and the turnstile unlocked to admit him into the garden on the other side.

Gardens were rare in Tcity, and on those few occasions when he came across them Will was always impressed by two features: the sky and the trees.

The open area of the garden meant that there was a wider gap between the surrounding buildings, and so the patch of sky overhead was more extensive than the long rectangular strips which followed the thruways.

The trees were made of stahlex and welded to the ground at equidistant nodal points. The branches angled from the stems with Euclidean precision in a series of abstract designs. Those who made a hobby of civic botany professed to be able to recognize the mannerisms of individual designers. They would have argued, for example, that the trees in this garden were of a different style from those which decorated the compound outside the Fun Palace or the Festival Hall. Will was always contemptuous of such sentiments, and maintained that one tree was indistinguishable from another.

He crossed the garden in a few strides, mounted a moving stairway, and was deposited in the Reception Area.

People were lounging about as if they'd been coming here for years, although the place hadn't been open more than a few weeks. A group of youths lazed in reclining chairs, holding long-stemmed glasses of pink liquor between finger and thumb, and turned their heads languidly to watch the passersby. They called to each other in loud, artificial voices, using the short vowels of the intellectual élite, with a suggestion of that American twang which was supposed to characterize the speech of Executives.

Will guessed that most of these people hadn't any intention of driving the autos. They simply wanted to be associated with the glamour and excitement of the new city facility. The Reception Area had become a species of preview to the First Sector, and had attracted a clientele similar to that which frequented the clubs and saloons which bordered Thruway 1.

A girl rubbed against him. He looked down into a pert face with empty, brazen eyes. She acknowledged his approving stare with a silver eyebrow and moved on, taking short steps inside a sharkskin sheath made from fine-gauge stahlex wire. The girl sat down in front of a wide tri-di screen, where yet another adventure of Princess Oriana was being shown.

Will regretted her absorption in the Oriana serial, but consoled himself with the thought that the sharkskin sheath made it impossible to tell from observation whether or not she was an aphrodolly. Besides there would be more, much more, of that sort of thing where he was going. In fact . . . yes, there it was again.

A girl with peculiar tubes on each side of a heart-shaped face was sitting on the other side of the Reception Area. She had just crossed and re-crossed her legs, before bringing together the sides of her wrap-round skirt, and the invitation had gone forth and been confirmed. It was as certain as a message from a semaphore, as bright as a signal from a heliograph. Only full graduates of the aphrocollege were qualified to wear flicker knickers.

Some change in Will's body-chemistry pumped him up with a feeling of euphoria. He felt as if he were floating. This was the new universe he had won for himself. Those hard-won increments had snatched him away from a life of mere sufficiency and given him this. And this was what it was about.

He groped in his pocket, withdrew a kickstick from a battered packet, and noticed an ornamental stahlex lighter on a nearby table. The device was a beautifully modelled auto, and the headlights burned with a red light when he picked it up. He lit his kickstick, exhaled the yellow smoke, and began to saunter round. It was good to savour a minor pleasure while postponing the major delights of the evening.

His eyes were attracted by a picture screen at which a number of people were staring. The oddity that excited attention was the antique nature of the pictures, which were two-dimensional and consequently seemed to lie flat on the wall. The first frame showed an artist's impression of the earliest auto – Cugnot's steam lorry; the next drawings were of Trevithick's steam carriage, and Otto's stationary four-stroke gas engine; the first motorcycle by Daimler was followed by the first motorcar of Benz; then came Butler's tricycle, with its twin cylinders and spark ignition; the French pioneers followed – De Dion and Bouton, Darracq . . .

It all seemed pointless to Will Forstell. Why did people want to drag up these old things that hadn't anything to do with anything? He turned away, and discovered he was looking into the face of the aphrodolly with the tubular shapes on the sides of her head.

'Fayre sir,' she said, 'mote I weete what straunge adventure doe ye pursew? From what I have espy'd my guess would bee that on these fresh-fangled autos ye have sette your harte?'

He recovered his composure. 'Yes. Yes, that's right. The new autos. But not the old things in these pictures.'

'Would ye dispute with Dionysius of Halicarnassus, who sayde in plaine wordes that historie is philosophie teaching by examples?'

He had no intention of disputing with anybody. Now that he looked at her more closely he saw that her hair had been grown into long plaits, which were coiled and confined in the silvered tubes of fretted stahlex on either side of her face. The tubes were suspended from a narrow stahlex band round the top of her head, in accordance with some old courtly fashion or other which he thought absurd. But the heart-shaped face between the tubes was enchanting, and now that he was close he could see a dimple in her pointed chin.

'I chiefly do inquere whether ye bee a goodlie wagoner, or whether like rash Phaëton, Apollo's son, you know not how to rayne the fiery chariot.'

'What's that you were saying?'

'In simple wordes, Sir Knight, doe you know how to stere aright and keepe an even course with yon autos?'

He laughed sharply. 'Yes,' he lied. 'Yes. Of course I do.

'Or mote ye in circles goe,' she persisted, 'like a silly wanton bird?'

'No. I know what I'm doing.'

Her shoulders were bare and white. Beneath them her breasts and torso gave shape to a dress of green silk, pulled tight down to the hips. A long row of closely spaced stahlex buttons began at the juncture of her collarbones and ended a little above the pelvis. The sleeves of her kirtle reached to her slender wrists, and long white streamers hung from her elbows.

'Doe ye now go across to that other sector of our city called the First, where men dream of nought but love and lustfull play?'

He nodded. 'They don't just dream of it over there.'

'Let me traveile with you when ye goe, and not be left a prey to foule reproches and disdainful spight. Do not leave me like a wofull, solitarie mayd.'

'I'm going over to have some fun,' he said, irritably. 'I'm not running a ferry.'

'And doe ye hope to bathe in wanton blis and bee Dame Pleasure's toy? Do ye think of tender breasts and daintie limbs, and even sweeter joyes?'

'Yes,' he said. 'All that sort of thing.'

'Then read my lookes, o elfin knight, and conceive of my intent.' To put the matter beyond any further doubt she pulled sideways at the heavy folds of her skirt, so that a vertical fitchet opened momentarily. The incandescent flicker winked at him.

'Yes,' he said again. 'What's your name?'

'Men call me Isabel.'

'That's a nice name. What's your scene?'

'I have a grove sette bye a chrystall stream. The entrance is a porch of rare device, formed by vines which overhead do arch and thrust their fatt grapes into the hands of those whoe enter in. Painted flowers make the aire drunk with their sweetnesse, and in a shadie glade we can laye us down and——'

'It sounds like my sort of place,' he interrupted. 'Let's go.'

CHAPTER TWO

Jan Caspol drove down to the causeway and headed towards the mainland.

Curlews and oyster-catchers were wading on the mud-flats. This was the route the pilgrims had used, twice every day at the ebb of each tide, to visit the island's shrine. Twice each day the sea had returned and washed away the prints of their sandals, as if to show the futility of all such devotions; or perhaps it showed that each act of devotion leaves an imprint which endures only a little while and must then be replaced by another. He opened a window and sniffed the salt, tangy air.

Big black-backed gulls wheeled against the iron sky. They were crying like lost souls, remembering the death of Aidan, keening for Oswald's severed limbs, lamenting Cuthbert's travelling bones. The northern sky above Lindisfarne still brooded upon the extinction of that primitive faith. Above the gulls, which continued to circle aimlessly over the black sea, he saw other birds flying on a straight course with purposeful wings.

'Fulmars?'

Sylvia followed the direction of his eyes. 'You're improving. They're heading for the colony on the Farne Islands.'

At the end of the causeway he turned left on to the autoway which followed the course of the old Roman road from Edinburgh to London. Holy Island and Lutyens's angled castle fell away behind them. He increased speed and locked in the co-ordinates. They passed the huge Norman keep of Bamborough, straddling its outcrop of igneous rock above the fierce waves that had brought the Danish pirates.

'Any second thoughts, Sylvia, about your expedition?'

'Of course not. You go and see Arthur Medway and forget all about me.'

He looked at her widely spaced grey eyes. The eyes alone, without the tone of her voice, would have convinced him of her steadfastness.

'People are more various than you think,' he said. 'Their faces don't fit the image you have of them.'

The road ran across a bridge with battlements and polygonal lookouts. A lion on the parapet growled leaden defiance at the deserted road.

'John Adam in his Gothick phase,' she said. 'Can we stop at the entrance?'

He resumed manual control and brought the auto to a gentle stop outside the massive barbican.

'Let's wait a few minutes, Jan.'

'Of course.'

He applied the secondary brake and there was the faint hum of a hydraulic pump lowering the parking struts.

'What's the matter, Sylvia?'

'I like to reinforce my sense of continuity, that's all.'

'We all do.'

They looked through the gigantic gateway which offered a view of the castle beyond. A cluster of angular bastions defended lofty walls, and were themselves defended by loftier towers.

'I like to think of the Percys running this place for four centuries. They ruled their little world for longer than we've ruled ours.'

'That's what people used to say about the dinosaurs,' he said.

'You missed a point, Jan. I expected you to say that we don't rule our world.'

'That's right. We don't *rule* it. We only *manage* it.'

He sensed the possibility of another argument on the old questions, and tried the diversionary tactic of releasing the brakes. The parking struts retracted and the auto rolled forward noiselessly.

'Managers have their responsibilities,' she said, 'just as the old rulers did. But the responsibilities of managers are harder to define because there aren't any divine sanctions for them.'

Sylvia had spoken with a hint of sadness and he looked at her quickly. Her grey eyes were fixed on the autoway ahead, and he knew she must be thinking of her self-imposed quest.

CHAPTER THREE

If you'd called for Osbert Osborne he wouldn't even have looked up from what he was doing. If you'd asked him about it, he would have had difficulty in remembering anyone who had ever used that name.

Anybody who wanted him, which wasn't very often, shouted for 'Ozzie'. Then he would respond immediately, but timidly, slowly and quietly.

Ozzie was a small man who somehow had the appearance of being smaller than he really was; and he imagined that he was even smaller than he appeared. His life had been uneventful. If you'd asked him about it, he wouldn't have been able to remember anything which had excited him; but here again, he imagined his existence to have contained fewer incidents than must occur in the life of any organism, no matter how lowly, so long as it breathes and moves.

He sometimes used to wonder what he did before he started work with Tcity Consultants in the Fourth Sector, but he could recall nothing before that date except an empty greyness which seemed to stretch backwards for ever. Sometimes he frightened himself (but only very mildly) with the thought that he might be some kind of robot which had been manufactured for the specific purpose of filing papers at the offices of Tcity Consultants. At such times he sought reassurance of his humanity by nipping the lobes of his ears until he could have cried with the pain. After that he would clench his hands, screw his eyes up tight, and with a final wrench of will direct himself to remember his previous life. There was nothing.

Nothing but an empty, grey, unmoving fog, in which he occasionally glimpsed his own features, as if through condensation on a mirror.

It might have been interesting if someone could have been instructed to scrutinize Ozzie's features, and then been subjected to questioning about what they remembered. The observer might have recalled that his hair was brownish, without being chestnut or coppery or auburn or reminiscent of the colour of anything else; that the hair was straightish without being either lank or wavy; that his eyes were bluish without having any hint of the sky or the sea; that his nose was neither large nor small, and that it wasn't hooked, or Roman, or Greek, or snub, or aquiline, or *retroussé*; that his mouth didn't turn up and didn't turn down, wasn't generous and wasn't mean, and served most of the time as a secondary breathing orifice.

It was altogether more probable that the observer wouldn't have been able to recall anything of a face which, to tell the truth, was one of the most unremarkable samples of physiognomy which ever went unremarked.

It's unlikely that Osbert Osborne, filing clerk, was closely observed by any of his fellow employees at Tcity Consultants. Not even by Mustapha, the head of Market Research, who noticed him sufficiently to bully him whenever he remembered to. Ozzie was neither good nor bad at his job. His duties were completely routine. He did what was required of him and not a tittle more. It never crossed his mind to wonder what people might do with the papers he gave them. For him it was simply a mystery, but it excited none of the curiosity which is normally associated with what is mysterious.

Occasionally he filed papers wrongly, and very occasionally he lost them. But he never made such an irretrievable mess of things that his function was investigated. His life was as anonymous as a name tag on a file that was never called for and gathered dust in some forgotten corner.

From time to time he would see Mr Amory, big and full of menace, striding towards him along one of the office corridors. Ozzie would flatten himself against the wall, breathless and trembling as a shadow, as Mr Amory swirled past.

Only once, and that very briefly, had Ozzie impinged upon the lives of his colleagues. The palms of his hands tingled with cold sweat when he thought about it.

The telephone rang in the Filing Department. One of the secretaries told him to come upstairs and collect some letters. Ozzie was still expressing compliance when the receiver at the other end was banged down. He went out into the corridor.

As he approached the foot of the stairs he became aware in his somewhat vague, abstracted way, that this area was packed with people. He noticed Mustapha elbowing his way about. After some hesitation, and a little reconnaissance, Ozzie found a narrow gap and turned sideways to slip through.

Rough hands seized him as he was raising his foot to the first step. For a dizzying second he didn't know where he was or what was happening. The ranks parted to permit the regress of his revolving body, and with a bone-jarring impact he found himself once again behind the disregarding backs. He was sitting down, staring at the blank wall of the corridor which fronted the steep stairway from which he had been so peremptorily diverted.

The blank wall served as a mirror to reflect the image which still burned and danced at the back of his eyes.

She had been almost at the top of the steep flight of stairs. Her legs, sheathed in their fine-gauge stahlex-wire stockings, glistened like the stalking limbs of some huge and predatory insect. When she reached the top step she leaned forward slightly, and displayed more of her intimate charms than the group at the bottom of the stairs could have ever hoped to see.

Or to see again. Because Tentrix, the girl from the Market Research Department, was Mr Amory's very private property.

Ozzie stood up slowly. The image which sparkled at the back of his mind fractured into a thousand parts, as if in sympathy with his shaken bones. Mustapha dispersed the crowd.

Ozzie placed an unsure foot once again on the first step of the precipitous stairway.

The sparkling picture of Tentrix re-formed in his mind, and hovered before him as he mounted the stairs. It was an image of dread. There was something about that pert face, and those brazen, empty eyes, which hinted at mysteries he didn't understand and didn't want to understand.

The others were always talking about her. They made jokes which he tried not to listen to. He wondered whether she might really be quite a nice girl who, because of the natural-seeming depravity of her face, and the obvious sensuality of her figure, provoked men to unburden their imaginations in obscene fantasies. No, he reflected as he plodded up the stairs, that couldn't be right. She must be wicked.

Mustapha started most of the stories about her. He said that when she wasn't occupied by Mr Amory she went along to the new Autoterminus in the Second Sector dressed in a long sharkskin sheath and tried to pass herself off as an aphrodolly. And it was notorious that she had lived in the Sixth Sector for a couple of years. You could tell that by her eyes.

Ozzie thought of the Sixth Sector and the cold sweat sprang into the palms of his hands again. Why did women go there? Hundreds of jokes were told about how women went there for pleasure. He remembered the stories. Some women went only now and again, because that was all they needed, or because the pleasure palled; some went only once, out of curiosity, and never went back. But some women went into the Sixth Sector and never came out again: they continued to live there like biological automata, hooked into some pleasure mechanism which enslaved their every reflex.

Tentrix reappeared when he was halfway to the top of the stairway, and he flattened himself against the stahlex handrail. For a second they shared a step together. He closed his eyes and clenched the banisters in his wet hands.

The stairway trembled, swayed, expanded in size until each step was two metres wide, then ten metres, then a hundred, then a thousand, and it continued to grow until he was stranded upon an infinite and featureless plain of desolation. He opened his mouth to scream, but no sound came out. Now the stairway began to shrink in size and its artificial horizon rushed towards him. An enormous wall advanced, decreasing in size as it came, so that it dwindled from the height of a beeblock to that of a man while it was still at arm's length, and it didn't stop shrinking until it froze at his feet in the form of the next step.

Tentrix had brushed against him.

He opened his eyes. She didn't so much as glance at

him as she continued on her downward progress. She hadn't even seen him.

Nobody ever saw him. He knew that. And there was additional proof of this phenomenon on the way home.

The crowd was so dense that he found it impossible to turn left into vestibule 713, which would have taken him to corridor 22 where he lived. He was carried onwards and in his panic turned right into a vestibule he didn't identify. At the next junction with a corridor he was forced to turn right again, and knew that he must now be going in the opposite direction to the one he wanted. Thoroughly disorientated, he took a left turn with the intention of zigzagging back through the intervening vestibules to corridor 22.

He wandered about in circles for a long time.

Someone in a hurry barged past and flung him aside with as little effort as if he were an inflated balloon painted in the semblance of a man. A flailing elbow caught him a little below the sternum. Ozzie doubled up, with one hand clutching his bruised stomach and the other scrabbling about the adjacent wall for something to hold on to. His searching hand fluttered across the handle of a module door, and his fingers closed around it like those of a drowning man clutching at a floating spar.

It soon became clear that such support wasn't needed.

There was some kind of blockage farther along the vestibule, perhaps because the man who'd barged past had tripped and fallen, bringing other people down with him; or perhaps it was due to an unusually large bottleneck where the vestibule debouched into the next corridor. Whatever the reason the crowd in front of Ozzie had stopped moving, and the people around him became more and more tightly packed as they tried to press forwards. The pressure on all sides meant that he couldn't have fallen down, even if he'd fainted. The same pressure made it impossible for him to maintain his doubled-up posture.

Slowly, painfully, Ozzie began to straighten up. His

stomach muscles contracted and pulled against his bent form like a bowstring, making him want to roll up in an anguished ball. But the pressure of people behind and in front was inexorable. His stomach muscles stretched, and he stood upright with tears in his eyes.

He looked down at his hand, which still grasped the door handle. He released it. He blinked to clear his eyes.

In the weeks to come Osbert Osborne would reflect that even the most uneventful lives are subject to great changes.

He would compare his life to a ship with a sleeping crew. The boat sails on its placid, unadventurous course, until it is diverted by some uncharted current or turned by some unexpected wind. It is only afterwards, when the new course is discovered, that it's possible to look back and say that so-and-so, at such-and-such a time, must have been instrumental in bringing about the change in direction.

It's never possible to say, at the time it is happening, that such a change is taking place.

And so it was with Osbert Osborne.

He looked through tear-filled eyes at the handle on the module door. It was in the form of a ring and had the natural brightness of polished stahlex. His tears diffused its glitter, turning it into a shining star, surrounded by silver mists and crowned with a halo of rainbow colours. Disbelieving, he slowly extended his fingers in the sparkling nimbus and felt the round shape in his hand.

He didn't know it at the time, but it was then that everything began to change.

CHAPTER FOUR

'The fields of Otterburn,' Sylvia said, gazing through the panoramic screen.

Jan hammered an iambic rhythm on the stahlex control panel :

> *'For Witherington needs must I wail*
> *as one in doleful dumps,*
> *For when his legs were smitten off,*
> *he fought upon his stumps.'*

'An inferior version of the ballad,' she said, 'rewritten for the broadside press.'

The auto murmured across the site of Morpeth where the heavy gateway of Dobson's Court House was carefully preserved. They passed the turning to Seaton Delavel. The very name conjured a picture of Vanbrugh's cyclopic hall, breathing contempt for Burlington villas in the effete south. Then the high, windowless walls of Tcity rushed towards them, rearing higher and higher until the auto entered their long shadows.

'No appointments in the Sixth Sector, I suppose?'

She gave him the highly disapproving look which she reserved for those occasions when he said something particularly tasteless.

They passed the autopark and North Gatehouse, and entered the tunnel under the Sixth Sector. The headlights came on automatically and bathed the ceiling and walls in white light. Jan accelerated, and the speed increased until they seemed to be rushing into the centre of a bright star.

'Tell me about some of the new things you've done,' he said.

She sighed. 'Some of them seem quite trivial, I'm afraid. For example, we've given names to the beeblocks.'

'So that the Citizens will feel more like people and less like bees?'

She ignored his sarcasm. 'And we've restricted the curfew when the scavenger system operates, so that they can move about more freely at night.'

He approved of that. In the days before he knew Sylvia . . . The curfew had made it difficult to get out of the First Sector late at night.

'But we've done some more interesting things. We've introduced a completely new city facility to let the Citizens drive autos.'

'Autos!' He sat bolt upright.

'They're manually controlled and they——'

'*Manually* controlled!' He was staring at her in disbelief. 'All you've got to do is read the history books and you'll see——'

She laughed at his astonishment. 'Let me finish, Jan. They are little electric cars running on batteries, and they're confined to a strictly limited road system between the First and Second Sectors.'

'Eeeee,' he said, wiping his brow and imitating the accent of the southern sectors in Tcity which had always delighted him. 'There were nowt like that when I were a lad.'

The auto left the tunnel and entered the open plain which lay between the black crescent of Tcity and the yellow sands of the pulverized shore. The castles fled behind: Lumley, with its square towers and machicolated turrets; and neighbouring Lambton, where the river Wear had carried the pieces of the monstrous Worm out to the North Sea. Another loop in the river showed where the cathedral had stood before it was removed to the north bank of the Colorado; and on the other side of the autoway was the site of Neville's Cross, where the northern barons fought for Queen Philippa.

'It used to be a hard land,' Jan said. 'Even the country houses were more like forts.'

She agreed. 'You couldn't write a history of castles without writing a history of Northumberland.'

A herd of red deer raised their heads as the auto passed. Beyond them a coniferous forest screened the enormous automated factories of the Stahlex Corporation, except for the fractionating tower which showed above even the tallest firs.

He drove into a side road, and again the auto ran into the shadow of lofty walls. It rolled to halt in the autopark outside the West Gatehouse.

Sylvia turned to him. 'Are you coming in?'

'I think I shall.' He applied the brakes. 'Even if it's only to refresh my eyes with Richard Wilson's sky.'

She opened the door, descended, and spoke to him across the curved roof of the auto. 'And your throat with Dixon's booze.'

'You shouldn't say things like that, Sylvia. You know how suggestible I am.'

Receptors in the door jambs identified the Executive hieroglyph, stamped into the ring of a Celtic cross which hung from Sylvia's neck by a fine chain. The door opened, and Jan followed her into the transit lounge.

'Good morning, madame. Good morning, sir.'

Dixon, who had obviously been waiting for them, bowed twice. The tails of his coat lifted like coleopteral wing-cases and the stripes on his trousers, even if extended to infinity, would have remained obdurately parallel.

'Hello, Dixon. How are you?'

'Very well, sir. I 'ope as 'ow you are the same.'

Dixon unnecessarily moved a wing chair a few centimetres in Sylvia's direction and she sat in it.

'Have you a copy of the schedule?' she asked.

Dixon produced a teletyped memorandum which she immediately studied. Jan crossed the room and looked at the Richard Wilson landscape.

'First I see Mr Felixtowe,' she read, 'who is the Director in charge of Depot Number One in the First Sector. He will pass me on to Mr Taggart, who seems to be a sort of general factotum at the same place. It's a pity that random selection should have chosen two people at the same depot.'

Jan was looking at the trees which framed the composition, and which were made to appear larger than they really were by the empty sky. The foreground was clearly delineated with a couple of detailed figures and pieces of masonry, behind which the middle distance was established by an ancient tower and woodland which followed the wide curve of a river. His eye followed the river until it was lost among placid fields and a horizon too far away for the distance to be guessed at.

'Then I see Mr Forstell,' she continued, 'who is Chief Clerk in the Stock Control Department at Depot Number Five. And finally I have an appointment with Mr Osborne, who is a filing clerk at Tcity Consultants in the Fourth Sector. It's a reasonable sample, I suppose.'

It was Claude Lorrain's basic compositional scheme, Jan decided, with its framework of balanced verticals and horizontals. The serene evening light had also been taken from Claude. Nevertheless the painting was quite clearly the work of Richard Wilson and nobody else. That was what the artists did. They climbed on to the shoulders of the men who'd gone before in order to see new perspectives, to discover new patterns in the scheme of things.

'I wonder if you would care to 'ave a taste of anything afore you go?'

The gatekeeper was looking at Sylvia, but Jan could tell from a sideways flick of the eye that the question was addressed to him.

'A good idea, Dixon. What have you got?'

'All the usual things, sir. And another crate of that white wine what the man as wrote the book about them musketeers said you 'ad to——'

'A bottle of that,' said Jan, with crisp decision.

Sylvia intervened. 'Half a bottle, Dixon.'

The gatekeeper hurried out.

Jan sighed resignedly, flopped into the companion wing chair, and stretched out his legs. Moderation in all things. It was the message of the room, too. He looked at the walnut furniture with its perfectly matched veneers, the video screen disguised as a Queen Anne wall mirror, the quiet reassurance of Richard Wilson's sky. He liked this room better every time he saw it. Perhaps he was losing his Romanticism and turning into an eighteenth-century man.

'The transit lounges in our gatehouses are aptly named,' he said. 'They are oases at the edge of a cultural desert. I'm glad that I'm not about to suffer such a jolting transition.'

'I shall find the transit bearable, Jan, provided I find some evidence that our efforts are causing the desert to bear some fruit. Even if it's only a lonely flower here and there.'

'But you've already tried.' He looked at her with some exasperation. 'What about the kickstick packets with pictures of cathedrals on them? What about the relays that spout Raphael Rozier's symphonies at every intersection of the thruways? What about the giveaway prints of Alençon's landscapes? What about——'

She waved her hand as if to sweep away a fly from somewhere in front of her face. 'All those methods were much too impersonal. We've realized that culture must be introduced to the Citizens as a truly living thing.'

'Of course.' He made an answering gesture with open palms, to indicate that such a conclusion was so eminently reasonable that only a maniac could disagree with it. 'But how are you going to do it?'

'The Central Executive have come up with some new ideas.'

'I know. You've told me some of them. But they don't seem very far-reaching to me.'

'We've got some others.'

Dixon came in with a cobweb on his ear, and half a bottle of wine and two glasses on a Paul de Lamerie tray. Jan busied himself with the wine and handed a glass to Sylvia.

'For example?' he asked, raising his drink.

'We've broadened the syllabus at the aphrocollege.'

Jan coughed, almost choked, and at the second attempt managed to swallow a mouthful of wine. 'Montrachet,' he gargled. 'As Dixon was about to remind us, Alexandre Dumas said it should be drunk on one's knees with the head bared.'

Dixon looked important, smiling from one to the other.

Sylvia was laughing gaily. 'Don't be absurd, Jan. You haven't forgotten your youth already. You remember the aphrodollies, don't you?'

'Of course I do.' He was recovering his composure. In the days before he knew Sylvia . . . He remembered one with brown skin, a necklace of sharks' teeth, and a red flower in her black hair.

'Well then. Instead of the aphrocollege simply turning out girls who conform with the desired gestalt criteria, as established by the libido profiles, we've ensured that each girl can project a relevant cultural gestalt.'

He swallowed some more wine, and managed to overcome another fit of coughing.

'Don't be so alarmed, Jan. The new graduates will continue to be efficient machines. But they will dispense cultural as well as sexual benefits to their clients.'

Jan shook his puzzled head. 'D'you mean a man might come across a woman who not only looks like Madame de Staël, but who talks like Madame de Staël?'

'Certainly.'

'What a double catastrophe!'

'You should be grateful,' she said, 'that things were so different when you were a lad.'

CHAPTER FIVE

Isabel took Will Forstell's hand in her small hot one, and led him across the Reception Area to a series of ticket dispensers which stretched the full length of one wall. He found that he was facing the dispenser farthest to the right which presented a picture at eye-level of a glittering silver object, shaped like a cigar with tall fins at the more tapered end.

Will thought it was some kind of spaceship, until he noticed that it had wheels on the underside and was therefore some species of luxurious groundcar. He lowered his eyes and read the cost of hiring one to drive over to the First Sector. That short journey would cost him all his increments for two months. He wondered if Isabel would notice how hot his own hand had now become.

'It is a goodly shape for to behould,' she said, 'and speaks high praise of the workman's witt.'

He made an indistinct noise and moved to the left.

The next panel illustrated a red vehicle, neither so long nor so low, with less elevated fins on the tail. It would have cost him six weeks' increments to go over in that. The next picture showed a blue auto with a somewhat square nose, and fins which were frankly rudimentary. It would have cost almost a month's increments.

'Unless false seeming doe beguile my eyne we backward goe, and all things grow less large,' she said.

'And less expensive,' he growled.

Will pulled her from one ticket dispenser to the next, her inertia increasing at every stage, until they faced the first panel at the beginning of the series. It showed a rectangular black box with a wheel at each corner, and open spaces where you would normally have expected doors.

'Now that's what I call smart,' he said.

She tossed her head, and imparted a swinging motion to the silvered tubes which adorned it. 'I would rather ryde upon a slouthfull asse, or on a filthie swyne with upblowne belly.'

'It's just the thing,' he contradicted.

In order to avoid the possibility of further debate he inserted his credit card in the scanning slot. She breathed in deeply, held her breath so long that it seemed the stahlex buttons must burst from her constrained bosom, and slowly breathed out again. After a brief whining noise a black card popped out of the machine. He picked it up and turned round.

'On the other syde,' she said in a defeated voice, and tugged his arm to turn him in the right direction.

He saw a directional sign which said *Autoexit* and walked over to it. The aphrodolly nudged him towards the barrier.

'Your ticket,' she said.

'Ticket?'

Isabel took the black card from his unresisting fingers and presented it to an alphanumeric scanner. A gate in the barrier opened. An electroluminous arrow switched on and off, on and off, directing them to a descending flight of stairs which led to the departure bay.

'There she is,' Will said, gesturing towards the squarish, if not quite square box which was waiting for them.

This application of the female gender, which came to him as if by intuition, established a new and complex relationship in which he, Isabel and the auto all had essential parts to play.

Indeed the feminine pronoun appeared to promote a more intimate relationship between man and machine in particular, because Will promptly forgot about the girl. He climbed into the vehicle, squeezed into the seat, and tried to make himself comfortable on the knitted stahlex upholstery.

A gathering of heavy skirts, and the intrusion of a white streamer, reminded him that he had a passenger. He looked about him, not at all sure what to do next.

'Now, Sir Knight, show what ye bee. Add faith unto your force and presse the starter button.'

He stared at the simple dashboard.

'The greene one,' she prompted.

He pressed a green button. There was a metallic whimpering and a refreshing smell of ozone. A vibratory motion was transferred to his back, his buttocks, and the underside of his thighs; a motion which, as soon as he placed his hand on the steering wheel, was transmitted to his shoulders and through them to his upper body.

'Now use your noble hand, Sir Knight, to restrain the handbrake's function.'

Will stretched back in his seat so as to be more certain of including the handbrake, whatever it was, within his field of vision.

'Ah me!' said Isabel. 'The signes be sadd.'

She reached forward, the white streamer floating from her elbow, and released the handbrake. Will, by stretching back in the driving seat, had unknowingly depressed the accelerator to some considerable extent. Consequently, with the brake off, the auto hopped away from the departure bay with the convulsive energy of a large black frog.

Once he'd overcome his astonishment, a doubtful happiness seized Will's spirit. Some mechanism smoothed out their jerky progress, and the auto began to proceed in a more orderly manner. His spirits rose further.

This was what life was about, he told himself guardedly, and started to sing. *Tra-la-la.* It was a catchy tune from one of Raphael Rozier's early symphonies, which had been given general currency by its use with one of the advertising lyrics of the Stahlex Corporation. *La-la-la.* He depressed the accelerator and the auto went faster. *Tra-la-la-lalala-la-la.*

'Doe ye like musick?' she asked.

'I sure do. *Tra-la-la-lalala-la-la.*'

She gathered the folds of the cote-hardie about her knees, tilted her head, and began to sing in a sweet voice:

'Ne cuidiez pas que le coeur ne me deuille,
Très douce dame, et que l'amoureux deuil
Moult durement ne m'assaille et accueille,
Quand je me pars de votre bel accueil . . .'

The strict design of the verse reflected the settled pattern of another way of life. Those limited and repeated rhymes were part of a limited and orderly universe, where each star moved in its appointed sphere and contributed to the greater harmony.

'Qu'à vos doux vis dire "à Dieu" ne puis mie:
Tant me fait mal de vous la départie . . .'

They were travelling along one of the exit tunnels from the terminus. Ceiling panels in the curved roof lit up and then switched off as the auto passed beneath them. The vehicle was thus preceded by a travelling band of yellow light which illuminated successive stretches of roadway, and was followed by blocks of darkness which slotted into place behind it.

Tra-la-la-lalala-la-la he sang.

The aphrodolly lay back with her eyes closed, and the soft melody of her voice invoked the European splendours of the Plantagenet courts. The words might have been listened to by Philippa of Hainault, thinking of her King at Crécy; or by the sad French lords, being waited upon by the Black Prince after Poitiers.

'Car quand je vois vos beauté non pareille
Et vos gent corps qui n'a point de pareil
Et vos fraîche couleur qui à merveille
Colorée est de blanc et de vermeil . . .'

A hundred metres before the end of the tunnel electroluminous signs flashed important messages. They instructed drivers to halt and give priority to drivers on the ring road, and then to proceed with caution in readiness for entering a traffic circle ahead. Will didn't see them. *Tra-la-la-lalala-la-la.* At the end of the tunnel were further directions for proceeding to different parts of the First Sector. He didn't see them, either. *Tra-la-la.*

The auto emerged from the tunnel as uncompromisingly as a cork from a champagne bottle. Owing to some random occurrence, which couldn't have had an average frequency of more than once every few months, there was a momentary gap in the traffic on the ring road. Will drove through the gap without being aware of it. *Tra-la.*

> '*Je n'ai vigueur ni sens qui ne m'oublie:*
> *Tant me fait mal de vous la départie . . .*'

The approach road to the traffic circle ran under a wide range of overhead signs, instructing drivers to take this, that, or the other lane, for this, that, or the other purpose. Will had time only to gawp at the unintelligible arrows as the auto sped beneath them.

He looked ahead. *Tra-la-la.* His disbelieving eyes saw hundreds of autos careering around the traffic circle.

Isabel continued to sing with her eyes closed:

> '*Ainsi partir et désir dont me deuil*
> *Me font languir en pëeur de ma vie:*
> *Tant me fait mal de vous la départie . . .*'

The unvarying refrain kept coming back like the memory of an image seen in a mirror. It was a song about a world where the various parts reflected the greater harmony of the whole. It was a self-consistent poem in a self-consistent universe.

Will found a pedal with his left foot, hoped it was a

brake, and pressed it as hard as he could. The auto slowed, rolled out of the approach road into the traffic circle, and stopped sideways on to the approaching traffic. He looked to the right. A red auto, with a radiator grille like the clenched teeth of a shark, was driving directly at him. Its headlights snapped white fury as it bore down upon its prey.

Will closed his eyes at the moment Isabel opened hers.

'Sir Knight,' she said, 'would it bee pleasing to your daintie eare if I mayde melodie with our Saxon tonge, such as oure rude Northumbrian bards did use?' She looked out of the auto and saw their predicament. 'You great stupid shit! What the hell are you doing?'

Her further words were drowned by the blaring of horns as the red auto swerved past. She continued to exploit the wide resources of the Saxon tongue, however, to a degree not usually considered proper in ladies of Angevin stock. The autos followed each other in rapid succession, swerving right and left to avoid the stationary vehicle, and flashing their lights in angry remonstrance. A medley of horns, hooters and klaxons made the air hideous.

Will continued to sit immobile. Twinges of cramp began to attack the calf of his left leg, which was already trembling with the strain of keeping the brake pedal depressed. He was gripping the steering wheel so hard that his fingers were numb. There was no way out of this impasse, so far as he could see, and he gazed with impotent dismay at the furious faces of the other drivers.

New pains commenced. He discovered that his passenger was kicking his ankles with all her force and drumming her fist into his ribs. The heavy folds of the cote-hardie partly muffled the assaults of her foot, but with every blow of her fist the white streamer at her elbow floated and curled in the air like a chivalrous standard waving from a battlement.

'Turn left!' she was yelling. 'Turn left, you bloody fool! You'll have us both killed.'

She managed to kick his left foot away from the brake pedal and hauled on the steering wheel as if her life depended on it – which indeed it probably did. The little black auto edged forward twice, and twice she had to stop it by applying the handbrake as other autos grazed around the square nose. At the third attempt Will managed to jump their auto into the traffic flow.

It was only now that the nightmare really started. A silver auto appeared from nowhere and overtook them on the left, so close that he couldn't understand how it hadn't ripped the side off. In surprise he veered to the right, where another auto was on the point of overtaking them, and it succeeded in doing so only after the sickening noise of stahlex sheets being scraped together.

'Drive straight!' Isabel shrieked.

From time to time he saw overhead signs, which seemed to indicate that there were ways of fleeing from this hellish maelstrom. From time to time, also, the aphrodolly screamed in his ear and pointed at exit roads. Whenever he turned the steering wheel, so as to aim at one of these escape routes, a blare of horns and a dazzle of lights made him straighten up and continue.

The other autos continued to pass on the right and left, in all shapes and sizes from the lordly silver missiles to other wretched black boxes on wheels. He felt himself to be despised, reviled and spat upon by all the world.

The torture continued. He winced at the blare of horns and flinched at the glare of lights. He feared all the other drivers more than he feared death because they made him die half-a-dozen times every minute. His arm and ankle on the passenger's side were covered in bruises. There was a singing in his ears, but it was no longer a *ballade* or *rondeau* by Guillaume de Machaut.

Will saw what he thought was an exit road. He half-turned into it before he discovered that the road was filled with autos approaching him two abreast.

'No entry! Halfwit!' The girl's imprecations wetted his ear as he swung the wheel back and drove on. 'I told you that the last time.'

Her final words caused a number of vague impressions to join together in his mind. Was it possible that he had some previous acquaintance with these landmarks? What about that side road over there, which joined his own route at such an oblique angle? Hadn't he seen it before?

'I've lost count,' her hoarse voice rasped in his ear, 'but I'd guess this is our tenth circuit.'

A new fear assailed him. 'We'll go round for ever,' he shouted. 'We'll just go round and round in a circle for ever.'

'No we won't, Sir Idiot. We'll come to a stop when the battery needs recharging.'

With muscles tensed, and the nape of his neck crawling, he began to edge the auto into the outside lanes of the traffic circle. Each circuit brought him nearer to the escape routes from the infernal whirlpool, and he determined to dive into the first one that fate offered him. He suffered imperious flashings in his driving mirror ordering him aside, and domineering blasts on horns instructing him not to wobble about, but eventually found himself outside the main traffic flow.

It was bliss to leave that murderous turmoil behind and return to the relative peace of the ring road.

The auto entered a tunnel and the ceiling lights charted its progress. Will applied the footbrake, and drove into a reception bay where the auto was finally brought to a halt by an opposing wall. He couldn't discover how to switch the engine off, so he left it running and climbed wearily out. He tangled his legs in some battery leads, kicked his way out of them, and didn't catch up with Isabel until he reached the barrier.

Will extracted his black ticket and presented it to the

alphanumeric scanner. The barrier didn't move and a red light blipped above the credit slot.

'What's the matter with it?' he complained. 'I've already paid.'

She replied through her teeth. 'You hired an auto for a trip from the Second Sector to the First.'

'I know I did. There's no need to——'

'Look around you, Sir Halfwit. We're back where we started, and you didn't pay for a return.'

Will dearly wanted to argue with somebody. The barrier remained closed, despite a vigorous shaking and kicking, and the red light continued to blip at him. He fumbled bad-temperedly for his credit card, dropped it, trod on his fingers, picked it up, and rammed it into the credit slot. After a brief whirring the barrier opened.

Isabel couldn't get away quickly enough for her liking. She pushed through the barrier in front of him, lifted the heavy folds of the cote-hardie away from her slim ankles, and hurried across the Reception Area to the seat she'd been occupying when he first saw her. As she swirled to sit down the insignia of the aphrocollege flickered like a homing beacon. She pulled the sides of her skirt together and the light was extinguished.

Once again she had become a figure of faery grace, and might have walked the green pleasaunce in an illustrated Psalter or a Book of Hours. Only her headgear gave any indication that her tranquil life had recently been discomposed. One of the stahlex tubes had somehow worked its way to the top of her head, and from its open end a plait of hair curled over her ear like a snake escaping from a jar.

Will Forstell crept away. He walked round the group of people staring at the picture screen of antique cars, and avoided the noisy youths drinking pink liquor from long-stemmed glasses. At his first attempt to leave the Reception Area he pushed desperately at a decorative wall panel, in the belief that it was a door. Hot with shame, he sneaked across to the exit.

His confidence in himself had been crushed to powder and blown away. In the days to come he would recall those fleering headlights and jeering horns, those shaken fists and angry faces. It hurt him all the more because he knew it was justified.

It had been an expensive day with no return.

'And I paid for a return,' he complained.

As he came out below the O of AUTOTERMINUS that suspended vowel seemed to express astonishment at his incompetence.

CHAPTER SIX

When the crowd started to move again Osbert Osborne moved forward with it. He didn't think of the door handle, to which he'd been clinging, in any conscious or specific way. When he reached the end of the vestibule, and clawed and kicked his way into the main corridor, he was aware only of a dim shape which glimmered in some dark corner of his memory. The light had faded to no more than a spark by the time he found his module.

As he was opening the door he paused, and looked down.

The spark in his memory was rekindled by some mysterious power, and the handle he was turning became transformed into a star-burst of white light. Even while he looked the light thinned into a grey mist and blew away into the unknown region whence it had come.

Ozzie was aware only of the stahlex handle in his palm, and the tips of his fingers sensing its curvature.

The handle on his module door was of quite different

design from that to which he had clung in the unknown vestibule. This handle wasn't in the form of a ring, but was more like a flattened S. This recognition of diversity serving the same purpose gave him an inexplicable pleasure.

The door opened, and the personal intimacy of the interior promptly isolated him from his recent experiences. He cracked his elbow against a shelf and felt that he was truly home.

'Damn you!' he bawled at the shelf.

The walls of the living-cubicle were featureless except for this shelf. The shelf was supported on a stahlex bracket, and in turn supported a lacquered vase containing artificial flowers and sprigs of schiaparelli. It wasn't often that Ozzie managed to get through an evening without bumping into the shelf.

He rubbed his long-suffering elbow and went about his various rituals as automatically as if they were reflex actions. First he pressed a button at random amidst the battery of such buttons which studded the frame of the tri-di. Second he turned to the autochef and, ignoring all the buttons embossed with specific recipes, he thumbed the one that said *Today's Surprise.* Third he crossed the narrow living-space and unfolded his cantilevered chair from the wall.

Plip!

The tri-di projected a three-dimensional image of a scantily dressed woman with golden hair. Ozzie recognized Oriana, the incredibly beautiful Princess who lived on the seventh planet of Sirius. She was the heroine of an unending serial in which she was wooed and worse by all the most eligible, and many of the most ineligible, bachelors in the galaxy.

Plop!

He went over to the autochef and discovered that *Today's Surprise* was soyjoy on toast. This surprised him quite a bit, because it was the same as yesterday. He picked up the plate disconsolately and lowered himself into the cantilevered chair.

Princess Oriana was about to undergo her lengthy and languorous ablutions. These activities habitually preceded an attempt, usually successful, upon whatever might be left of her honour.

She discarded the last of her open-knitted stahlex-wire underwear, and with slender legs stepped into a bath shaped like a scallop shell. The inside of the shell was the colour which had once been euphemistically described in the charts of interior decorators as 'intimate pink'. This soft pinkness was reflected through the translucent water upon the softer contours of her body, and gave her rounded flesh an added roseate glow.

Now the Princess moved her hands about in the water, slowly and caressingly at first, then faster and faster. She created a turbulence of excited bubbles which lay like froth on a wind-blown wave, and which multiplied with every movement of her hands until their sparkling spheres clung to her neck and breasts like jewels.

Ozzie was sitting with the dish on his knees, poking morosely at the soyjoy on toast with a stahlex fork. These recurring preambles to the real action in the Oriana serial were like the preludes in advertisements put out by the Stahlex Corporation. Whenever the screen projected a girl pulling on a pair of fine-gauge stahlex-wire stockings, you could be sure that the door would open to reveal a young man with natural hair and a hand-stitched suit.

The door opened to reveal a tall man, mightily shouldered and deep of chest, with a massive corded neck and heavily muscled limbs. He was clad in silk and velvet, but the great sword at his side seemed more natural to him than those rich accoutrements. The brow was low and broad, and the eyes smouldered as if with some volcanic fire. His dark, scarred, almost sinister face was that of a fighting man, and his sumptuous garments couldn't conceal the hard, dangerous lines of his limbs.

'Coonan! Coonan!' moaned Oriana in ecstasy.

'Loonan! Loonan!' groaned Ozzie, sucking the last of the soyjoy from his stahlex fork.

'I pray every day that you will come,' Oriana cried, rising from her scallop shell.

'I pray every day you'll smack her bum,' Ozzie sighed, rising from his cantilevered chair.

He made his way to the disposal chute, empty dish in hand, and again cracked his elbow against the shelf but much more resoundingly than before. The dish slipped through his fingers.

'Damn you!' he shouted at the shelf. 'Damn you! Damn you!'

He swept the lacquered vase from the shelf and it bounced half-a-dozen times on the floor with a metallic *pinggg*, rising to such a height on each occasion that the laws of gravity appeared to be temporarily nullified. At the first leap the artificial flowers jumped out, and with a few sprigs of schiaparelli arranged themselves in a floral tribute on the soyjoy-stained dish.

Ozzie returned his attention to the shelf, and wrenched impotently at the supporting bracket until its stahlex frame cut his fingers.

'Think you're clever?' he enquired. 'I'll soon show you whether you're clever or not.'

He pawed at a wall panel and it slid sideways to reveal a cupboard which was wide but shallow. The congeries of odds and ends thus revealed always depressed him. He poked about, and immediately dislodged two empty stahlex beer cans which *tinggged* on the floor and rolled away in a game of follow-my-leader. A Neochristian Adventist tract entitled *Prepare Ye The Way* shuffled itself to the top of the junk and fluttered to the ground. A few of its pages turned, of their own volition, as if to provide a quick refresher course in the reinterpretation of Isaiah, Chapter XL.

Ozzie began to imagine that the stuff in the cupboard was ganging up to frustrate his endeavours. His groping hands encountered something with arms, and he dragged it out into the light.

It was a long white jacket, so long that it reached below his knees, with vertical black stripes. He'd bought it some time ago, in the belief that it would make him look taller. He hadn't worn it after the first day at work, when Mustapha had come into the Filing Department and said he looked like a monkey starving to death in a cage. From some fold of this garment there now fell the object of his search.

The small cylinder bore the legend *Meltstahl*. On one side of the tube were directions for its use. He already knew how to use it, through having applied it to a coat peg which used to be fixed inside his module door, and which had irritated him unbearably after he stopped wearing the striped jacket. On the other side of the tube, in miniscule print which he'd never read to the end, and which he knew he wouldn't understand if he did, was an explanation of how Meltstahl worked. All he could remember was that it had something to do with splitting the crystal lattice at the interface between stahlex components.

Ozzie returned to the shelf, held the cylinder nozzle against the junction of bracket and wall, and squeezed. A globular mist exuded from the self-sealing aperture, condensed at the point of application, and began to disappear. He gave it another squeeze, just to be sure, and pocketed the cylinder.

He stood back a pace and regarded the shelf with a smile of superior menace. In a previous age a schoolteacher might thus have regarded a small boy whom he was about to chastise.

Ozzie gripped the supporting bracket and pulled. It came away from the wall with a sharp report, somewhat like a broken icicle. He lifted the bracket to his eye. The part which had been fixed to the wall had a granulated surface, showing where the Meltstahl had crept into the crystal structure and opened the interface. .

He chucked the bracket, with the attached shelf, into the disposal chute. Then he dusted his hands, one against the other, in the immemorial tri-di gesture of a man who has finished a job and is proud of it.

A movement caught his eye and he turned towards the screen.

He'd missed the climax, but didn't regret it. If you missed one you missed them all.

Princess Oriana lay on the crumpled silken coverlets of her divan. Her white arms curved limply above her head, her half-lowered lids turned her eyes into liquid half-moons, and a soft smile of remembered pleasure dimpled her mouth. Coonan sprawled beside her, and as you looked at his corded neck, his mighty chest and hairy limbs, you remembered that this was the barbarian who had hacked his way to lordship through flame and blood.

The Princess became playfully amorous once more. She nibbled Coonan's ears. She entangled her fingers in the black mane of his hair, pouted her mouth for a kiss, and pulled his face towards hers.

His face came off.

Princess Oriana, her mouth stretched wide with horror and disbelief, stared at the wrinkled mask in her hand. Slowly she raised her eyes, and looked into the face of the creature which had so foully exploited her love for Coonan. She screamed.

It was an ape-man. He had come from the planetary system which circles around the dark-eclipsing variable star which Arabic astronomers had named Algol, or the Demon. Now the ape-man was amorous, too, and he wasn't being playful. She screamed again.

Ozzie switched the screen off and went into his sleeping-cubicle. He'd never been able to understand Princess Oriana.

CHAPTER SEVEN

Taggart pushed his way out of Thruway 1 into a side-street. His shoulders were hunched, and his head hung between them like that of an animal which strives in vain to escape its pursuers. He was a special kind of animal, and he was being hunted by demons which could never tire or be thrown off the scent.

Oh God! Oh God! Let him not remember!

His mother's face shone down the passageways of his mind like a white lamp suspended in the crypt of some black and stinking catacomb. He saw her rounded cheeks, and the fair hair curling over the tops of her small ears; her tall brow, as smooth and clear as a mirror; and her wide eyes, of a blue so faint and transparent that they might have been mere windows through which her pure spirit could look out at the unintelligible world.

She had a tiny nose, as unobtrusive as herself. Her mouth, too, was small like that of a child, with a short top lip and a lower lip which trembled except when they were alone; and sometimes even then.

To Taggart his mother had always presented the same picture. No matter what part of their life together he recalled, he saw the same ingenuous eyes in the same unchanging girl's face. Perhaps she was one of those people whose faces change so slowly with the passage of the years that you don't notice. Then he reminded himself that he'd lived with his mother for only a few years. Her face didn't have time to change although her body . . . he closed his eyes . . . although her body . . .

Taggart threw himself into a scrum which swayed and heaved at the beeblock doorway. He used his elbows and knees with more than customary vigour, in the hope that this surplus expenditure of energy might drain away some of the sickly fluids which were feeding his memory.

How far back into childhood could the memory go? Perhaps his earliest conscious memories of his mother were from the time when he was three or four years old. Those memories were no more than cloudy images overlaid with later impressions of a rounded face and fair, curling hair. He wished with all his heart that he could remember the earlier times. It was unbearable to consider that those first years had disappeared just as if they had never been. Yet they had existed, and he could have cried with anguish to think that they were no longer accessible to him, no longer recorded in any form which could make them live again in his imagination.

Taggart knew with as much certainty as if he had recorded every scrupulous detail that those first years were ones in which his mother had protected and cherished him with every device she could command.

He supposed that most people's earliest memories existed in a kind of grey fog, where half-recognized figures drifted by on forgotten errands. He had vague recollections of lying awake in his cot, listening to the noises coming from the living-cubicle, and he guessed that these memories were amongst his earliest. The noises from the living-cubicle were strange, and he wasn't able to connect them with anything he knew. It was only later that the noises made pictures appear in his mind.

The first time the pictures appeared he cried out in horror. He cried out again and again until his mother came in . . .

Taggart directed his eyes to the electroluminous signs which glowed in the ceiling of the corridor. He tried to concentrate all his faculties on shuffling into the right lane for the levator station.

When his mother came in she was wearing some kind of coat buttoned tightly up to her neck. When she leaned over his cot to whisper her reassurance, he flung his arms round her neck and pulled with all his might to bring her face next to his on the pillow. He discovered that her cheeks were hot and wet with tears. What surprised him more was the way her body resisted him when he tried to pull her down to him with his small arms. She was stiff, reacting like a spring, and when he held her tight she flinched in his child's embrace.

Taggart flinched as he remembered. He scrambled forwards, unaware of the kicks and flailing arms of his competitors for the empty levator chamber.

His mother had sung him to sleep while she stroked his forehead. Her voice was as soft and high-pitched as a child's, but full of sorrow.

He would have given his eyes in return for being able to recall those songs. Sometimes a tune on the tri-di, perhaps an advertising jingle put out by the Stahlex Corporation, would stir indefinable things in his memory like an air-blower whirling debris along the city corridors; sometimes he imagined that he could recall a couple of notes, and that with a little more concentration he would be able to reproduce a snatch of melody or a few words: but when he tried to lay hold of them the elusive patterns of sound disappeared, like reflections glimpsed in water.

Sometimes he feared that these intangible things weren't memories but only vain imaginings; and that his mother had never come into the cubicle and never sung to him: but he knew, beyond the need of proof, that the indescribable sweetness which lingered in his memory was some kind of distilled essence from the songs his mother had sung to him.

And behind the sweetness of the memory was the droning monotone of the other woman speaking, and the harsh inflection of his father's voice.

His father . . . The levator door clashed behind him but the chamber lights didn't come on. Taggart stood in the darkness, and tried to hold his breath against the stench of the crowded bodies. His father . . . Oh God! Oh God! Let him not remember!

His father was a small man, with narrow shoulders and a pinched chest. Yet in some way he gave the impression of being very strong. This illusion, if it was an illusion, was made to appear more real by his hands. They were so disproportionately large it seemed scarcely possible that the tendons to operate them should be contained in his skinny wrists.

The face was long, with extraordinary eyes. The irises were so large that the whites of his eyeballs were apparent only when he looked askance. The irises, moreover, were of a brown so dark as to be almost indistinguishable from the pupils, so that his eyes looked like wet black grapes. Had it been possible to disregard the rest of his face, the eyes could have been those of a mischievous dog.

But it was impossible to view the eyes in isolation because they, like every other feature, were dominated by the mouth. His father's mouth was thin, constantly wet with spittle, seeming to sneer at some secret knowledge which he alone possessed; and it imbued every line and wrinkle of that narrow face with the character of its own malevolence.

The levator stopped with its usual abruptness and the door clanged open. Taggart was spewed out into the corridor, and clutched at the person in front to maintain his balance.

How had his father managed to maintain his balance in these seething city corridors?

His father's left leg had been maimed, either at birth or in some accident, so that it was permanently cranked and dragged along behind his other leg. He walked, or rather he proceeded, by sinking briefly on to the ball of his splayed left foot, quickly extending his other leg, then rocking forward on to his right foot and trailing his crooked leg behind him. When Taggart remembered the way his father walked, the jerking image was accompanied by a recurrent scraping noise, as if the dead foot were equipped with claws.

How could his mother have loved such a man?

As Taggart shouldered his way along the corridor he recalled stories of women who had been attracted to men with deformities. There were cases of women being obsessed by dwarfs, hunchbacks, cripples and monsters of different kinds. A deformed leg might suggest the cloven hoof of a satyr or devil. Princess Oriana had once happily submitted to the multiple caresses of a six-armed giant from Alpha Centauri, until she was forcibly rescued by Coonan.

Taggart flung such thoughts away in horror, and turned off into the vestibule where he lived.

His mother had been an angel. She was as incapable of such inclinations as she was of visiting the women's pleasure palaces in the Sixth Sector. Perhaps she had paired with such a beast because she felt sorry for him. And what was done, was done. She had stayed with him like a good and faithful wife of the olden times. And yet there were things . . .

Taggart reached the door of his module. He opened it quickly and stepped inside. The total absence of other people, the absolute silence, made him light-headed for a moment.

And yet there were things which made it incredible that his mother should have stayed with his father as long as she did. His father's body was ugly and crippled, but it was beautiful and straight compared with his mind.

Taggart groaned and unfolded a seat from the wall. Now his memories had him on the rack, and the evening stretched before him like a torture chamber of infinite resource and ingenuity. He heard the droning monotone of the other woman speaking, the harsh inflection of his father's voice, his mother's sobs, and the strange, sharp sounds which made the pictures jump into his mind.

CHAPTER EIGHT

On his left were the York Moors. The upper reaches of their limestone skeletons were thinly clothed in heather, but lower down were rich valleys where fat sheep browsed. These were followed by the chalk scarps of the York Wolds, where root crops for animal foodstuffs flourished in the glacial clay.

The auto ran on into the plain, and fields of wheat undulated in its wake like waves behind a ship.

Away to the right and swathed in mists the Pennines sprawled like a dead giant fallen on his face. His fleshless back was hunched against the northern sky. The broken vertebrae looked like battlements on a monstrous fortress, built for defence against some forgotten race. Down below, where his splintered ribs had taken root in the earth, the carcase was invaded by the deep, lush vales of Yorkshire, and sleek cattle wandered there.

The granary and larder of the Executives, Jan Caspol reflected. We live in a style that would have made the Medicis feel like the meanest beggars outside their palace gates.

The panoramic window showed an empty, rolling plain, and unspoiled countryside, where ancient industries had at one time dominated a bleak landscape. Up there, between the river Aire and the river Calder, West Riding woollens and worsteds had prospered before synthetic materials replaced them; here, less than a thousand metres below the autoway, were the seams of the concealed coal-field which were far from exhausted even when natural gas became the prime source of energy; there, around the banks of the river Don, iron and steel had been manufactured in the days of open towns and cities; and over there, just north of the river Trent, had been the home of lace and hosiery before the development of man-made fibres.

Now it had all gone. Not only the ancient industries –

woollens and worsteds, coal mining, iron and steel, lace and hosiery – but also the industries which had replaced them. The products of the Stahlex Corporation provided for almost any requirement, ranging from the massive plates which armoured city walls to the incandescent hair-fine wires used in flicker knickers.

Jan smiled, not altogether happily. If he were perfectly honest, he would have to admit that he preferred the casual warmth and comfort of his stahlex-knitted jerseys to the hairy elegance of the Harris tweed he was wearing. But dare he admit as much to Sylvia? The Harris tweed had been a present from her. She had used her influence with the City Executive of Clydecity to have the jacket made by crofters on Lewis.

His stahlex-knitted jerseys and the tweed jacket, he thought, represented the horns of the Executive dilemma. Was the Work Project the real solution to the problem, or was it merely a return to barbarism? The jerseys were computer-designed and made on automatic machines from raw materials which cost virtually nothing. The tweed jacket, on the other hand, must have been enormously expensive in real terms, requiring more human skill and labour than the manufacture of the auto he was driving.

How much of the past should they preserve? It wasn't simply a case of maintaining a late Norman chancel because it contained a particularly fine example of the waterleaf motif in its capitals; or deciding to knock down half-a-dozen Pele towers because there were better specimens elsewhere. It had to do with something much more important but much less easily described.

It had to do with deciding how much of the past it was necessary to preserve if ordinary people were to retain an experience of continuity and a sense of purpose. Sylvia was probably right. The universal culture of the Executives, their global *Kulturgesicht*, gave them this sense of continuity and purpose. But the Citizens needed something different. Such as the Work Project? And the supporting facilities recently introduced on the advice of the Central Executive?

These were the questions, explicit or implied, which lay behind so much of their conversation in recent days. The questions hadn't been far away when they were talking over dinner the previous evening.

Jan had spent the afternoon in the sun lounge. He was dividing his attention between the first volume of Alençon's *Journal*, which lay open on his knee, and observing the activities of their small son who was playing in the garden.

Sperry was only a year old, but clearly recognizable as a child of the Executive class. The sides of his head swelled above the ears, and the scars which indicated surgery on the temporal lobes hadn't yet faded. His shoes were of doe-skin, with stahlex snap-clasps, and would have cost a Citizen a year's income. His cardigan was hand-knitted, in a yarn spun out of fleece plucked from the necks of vicuñas. A strange irony, Jan thought: the wool which had been a luxury strictly reserved for Inca chiefs, and which would have disappeared but for the decrees of Simón Bolivar, now clothed a child who would inherit privileges undreamed of in Peru.

And yet Sperry was only a human baby, after all.

He was walking, with unsteady and too-eager steps, along the unevenly paved footpath which skirted the herb garden. In one hand he clutched a yellow stahlex bucket, and in the other a yellow stahlex spade. On an impulse he stopped, and began to dig furiously among Sylvia's aromatic plants.

After a good deal of effort Sperry managed to make a small stone and some loose earth stay on the spade long enough for him to transfer them to the bucket. That done, he leaned over until his nose was touching the rim of the bucket, and peered steadfastly into the interior. When he had assured himself that the materials he'd just deposited were truly there, he returned to his digging.

Jan returned to his book. It was in the form of a diary kept by the last of the great painters before the Denaissance.

If I could be granted one wish, Alençon had written, *it would be once again to see everything around me through the eyes of a child without sacrificing my adult intelligence. It would be like waking up on another planet which was near to bursting with the variety of unimaginable creatures and incredible flowers it contained.*

He looked up from the book. Sperry had made some more flourishes with the spade at a greater distance and captured a few bits of orris root flavoured with a sprinkling of thyme. He transferred these also to the bucket, and examined them in their new habitat. Sperry, his nose touching the rim of the bucket, squeaked with triumph.

Jan's heart ached in sympathy with that childish triumph. It was Sperry's first insight into the universe which Newton had invented. When you put an inanimate object in a secure place it stayed there, and didn't fly away. It had been a self-consistent universe, rational and harmonious.

A plump thrush ran on to the path, seized a worm, and started to jerk it from its hole. Sperry dropped his bucket and spade, and hurried forward with a cry of alarm. The thrush flew up with the worm dangling from its beak, but dropped it in mid-flight and disappeared into a neighbouring bush.

Jan closed the book.

Sperry bent solicitously over the worm, and after great deliberation picked it up and carried it back to its hole. The worm showed no signs of wishing to re-enter its home. Sperry tried to push it in, and spoke inarticulate and coaxing words to it, but the worm wouldn't co-operate.

Jan lit a felicity, inhaled deeply, and observed his son through the mauve smoke.

The child's smooth face showed painful concern. He didn't want to hurt the worm, or even make it do anything it didn't want to do; yet he was convinced that the worm should go back into its hole if it was to be happy and safe. So he continued to push the end of the worm into the hole, torn by the conflict between doing what he knew to be right, and yet terribly anxious not to cause any distress.

A chime sounded from the castle. It tinkled in the clear air like a cowbell.

Jan left the sun lounge and went out into the garden. Sperry looked up, ran across to take his hand, and pulled him away to look at the worm, chattering all the time about his recent adventure.

'You've done everything you can,' said Jan, nodding sagely at the immobile worm. 'All you can do is point people in the right direction, so that they can see which way to go. But what they actually do is up to them.'

He threw his felicity away and they walked hand-in-hand up the ramp to the castle. The cobbles were laid in Lutyens's herring-bone pattern, and Sperry found them tiring to walk upon. He consented to being picked up when they were almost at the top.

Sylvia appeared in the entrance hall, and expertly relieved Jan of his sleepy burden. Jan kissed her forehead, and stepped down into the passage which took him past the dining-room.

At the end of the passage was what they still called the 'Ship Room', although the model in full rig had long since been detached from the ceiling and thrown away. He went straight to the dispenser and thumbed the vermouth button.

He sipped the bitter-sweet drink, sniffed and sipped. The Executives of Pocity had changed it again! Why did they keep fooling around with yet another mixture of

Alpine simples in their Piemontese wines? He took a larger swallow, and set the glass down on one of the semicircular Flemish tables which stood on either side of the dispenser.

In many ways this was the pleasantest part of the day. He'd spent the early morning in bed listening to music, then an hour or so in his systems lounge to ensure that all was well with the operations of the Stahlex Corporation; a light lunch was followed by a game with Sperry; then desultory reading in the sun lounge until the air became cold. Now the day was behind him, and he was looking forward to an evening with Sylvia.

Jan drank some more vermouth, and looked out through the window embrasure at the grey waters of the North Sea. We are fortunate people, he thought. We are the most fortunate people who ever lived.

We are the first race of men which hasn't had to spend most of its waking hours in economic toil, either through necessity or through desire for luxury. At the same time we aren't demoralized by idleness, or isolated from economic processes as privileged minorities used to be. We each have a specific Executive responsibility, just as I have for the Stahlex Corporation and as Sylvia has for Tcity. By spending an hour or two each day in our Executive functions we satisfy our need to feel that we are making some contribution to human welfare.

In addition, we are more intelligent than any men who ever lived. Gene surgery and post-natal amplification of the temporal lobes have made us capable of deeper intellectual pleasures than were available to previous men. Extra intelligence adds an extra dimension of pleasure to everything we do.

There were disappointments and doubts which the Executives continued to endure. For example, creative ability seemed to have died, and they had entered a period which art historians had labelled the Denaissance. The Executives had an incomparable grasp of total world culture, but they were wretchedly aware that they wouldn't leave any culture of their own. Also, it wasn't clear how far their moral sense had advanced with the increase in their intellectual powers. There were those who said that there had been no moral progress at all.

Jan drained his glass and looked out at the grey waters of the labouring sea. In his view the single fact that the Executives hadn't degenerated, despite their unlimited authority and freedom, was in itself a proof that there had been some ethical progress. Would any previous élite, as secure in its privileges and power as the Executives, have bothered about the happiness of the Citizens?

He returned to the dispenser and filled his glass. Sylvia bothered about the happiness of Citizens in Tcity all the time. As City Executive she was expected to implement the policies of the Central Executive, but it went further that that. She was committed to the welfare of Tcity by some dictate from her own spirit, far more powerful than any external directive.

Jan didn't agree with all her views of human nature, but he was glad of her devotion to the Work Project and its associated programmes. He shamefully admitted to himself that perhaps he was glad because she made amends for his own less morally fine nature. Personally he tried not to think too much about the Citizens, as if not thinking about them would make them disappear. The solipsist fallacy, he concluded, as he sipped his drink.

Sylvia came in and looked at the half-empty glass in his hand. 'Your second,' she asserted, with mock severity.

He avoided the issue. 'What kept you?'

'Sperry wanted something to eat. I sometimes think he must eat his own weight several times a day. Like a bird.'

Jan thumbed the vermouth button. 'You'd better not let him hear that analogy.'

'Why not?' she asked, taking the drink.

He related their son's adventure with the thrush and the worm.

'Sperry already observes the First Precept,' she commented.

'The First Precept?'

'The First of the Five Precepts of Buddha!' She blinked astonishment at his not grasping the reference immediately. 'The Fifth Precept, by the way, says you mustn't drink.'

'And despite his father,' Jan said, 'Sperry is a *bu*dding *Bu*ddhist.' He gave the repeated 'b' and 'u' sounds their full explosive force in the accent of the southern sectors.

Sylvia sipped her vermouth.

'Spe*rr*y is a g*rr*owing gu*rr*u,' he added, rolling the 'r' in the Tcity manner.

'They've changed it again!' she said. 'Too much coriander.'

'A developing Dalai Lama,' he persevered, using the sing-song intonation of the northern sectors.

Sylvia put her unfinished drink on the nearer of the Flemish tables. 'I've always considered the Buddha's Eightfold Path to be one of the best strategies for a good and happy life. I'm sorry you're so flippant about it.'

'I'm not flippant. It's just that I don't like some of the Precepts.'

She made a move towards the dining-room. 'Which ones,' she asked over her shoulder, 'apart from the Fifth?'

'I don't seem to remember the others at the moment.'

He swallowed the remains of his vermouth, pushed the empty glass into the disposal chute, and followed her.

'Jan, why don't you drop me off at the West Gate tomorrow? Then while I'm conducting my interviews you can run down to Allington Castle and refresh your memory.'

'What's at Allington?'

'The Executive Vihara.'

He smiled vacantly.

'For goodness' sake, Jan, it's our Buddhist monastery!

You'll meet Arthur Medway there. I'm sure you'd like him.'

He pulled out a chair for her and kissed her cheek. 'If you're still determined to have your interviews, I promise to think about it.'

He sat down opposite to her.

'I'm afraid I didn't programme anything,' she said. 'It's only the *plat du jour*.'

Jan forked a few rosy sword-shrimps, boiled in filtered sea water and encased in aspic jelly. He sniffed the wine, and swallowed a good mouthful.

'Muscadet,' he said. 'The favourite wine of Abélard and Héloïse.'

Sylvia laughed. 'No evidence whatsoever for the second statement. You're an incurable Romantic.'

He couldn't have denied it. He'd been a Romantic since the day in early adolescence when he had read the first canto of Byron's *Childe Harold*. Ever since then he'd felt himself at heart to be an early nineteenth-century man.

Sylvia had an eighteenth-century mind. Her intelligence had the rounded elegance of a couplet by Pope, the balanced harmony of a string quartet by Haydn, the geometric logic of a painting by David, the proportions of an entablature from Vitruvius. Of the eighteenth century Jan liked best those features of it which seemed to anticipate the spirit of Romanticism: James Thomson's *Seasons*, John Dyer's *Grongar Hill* and Edward Young's *Night Thoughts*; the second movement of Mozart's G minor symphony, and the ghostly trombones which preceded the entry of the stone guest at Don Giovanni's supper; the black and white chalk sketches of Gainsborough which breathed a fresher air than he ever captured with his brush.

Jan preferred those aspects of the eighteenth century which had, in one way or another, betrayed that spirit of rationality for which Sylvia so much respected it. When she quoted an eighteenth-century philosopher, he usually responded with one of the more extreme utterances by a nineteenth-century poet: which didn't prevent her from asserting that there was inside him an eighteenth-century man trying to get out.

'Let's see what we get next,' she said, and pressed the console button.

Jan touched the ends of his fingers together. 'For what we are about to receive, may we be truly thankful to the Central Services Department.'

The main course came forward: pré-salé mutton, fattened on the aromatic pastures of salt meadows in Britanny. The well-fleshed breasts had been prepared and grilled in the manner perfected by Antonin Carême at the court of St Petersburg, and were served with devilled sauce seasoned with cayenne pepper.

He pushed the not-quite-empty bottle of Muscadet into the return slide, and thumbed a button which brought forth an uncorked Château Stahlex-Joinville-Robert.

Jan emptied his glass and immediately refilled it.

'I must have some energetic Buddhist chromosomes,' she said, 'for them to withstand the onslaught of your Bacchanalian ones in poor Sperry's inheritance.'

'They must fight like Trojans,' he said.

'You are lacking in a "cool self-love".'

'I know. "Damn braces. Bless relaxes."'

It was a strangely endearing thing about Sylvia that she so much esteemed the minor figures among the eighteenth-century philosophers. She looked to them for advice on how to live, and not to the great names of Hume, Kant or Hegel. Thus she contended that an understanding of what the third Earl of Shaftesbury meant by 'benevolence', and what Joseph Butler, Bishop of Durham, meant by 'cool self-love', would have reduced, and could still reduce, much of the unhappiness caused by a Romantic temperament.

'Coffee-house moralists!' he said.

'Our solar system is a coffee-house, Jan. Perhaps it is

only a corner table in a coffee-house, and so isolated that people at the other tables haven't even noticed it. It's a comical impertinence for any of us to attempt the construction of a metaphysical system.'

He objected. 'You can't justify ethical codes unless they are part of a metaphysical system.'

Cruising south on the autoway to Allington at 250 kph, Jan Caspol recalled their conversation and smiled. Highly as Sylvia thought of Shaftesbury and Butler, she respected the work of Yutaka Kimura even more. He wondered how far she would succeed in explaining Kimura's industrial psychology to the Citizens of Tcity.

CHAPTER NINE

'You don't remember Steve, do you?' asked Gloriana Schnurrbush.

Dab rubbed his chin against her bony knee and blinked his big Landseer eyes to show that he was listening.

'Of course you don't. You couldn't possibly remember him. You didn't come along until after my Steve had gone off and . . . had gone away.' She adopted a more confidential, a more intimate tone. 'Did I ever tell you how we first met?'

Dab brought his ears forward and limply wagged his tail, to indicate that although he'd heard it all before he was prepared to listen to it all again. He would have to, anyway.

'We met in the levator going up from Floor 87 where we are now. There now! Isn't that romantic? Naturally everyone is most surprised when I tell them how it happened.'

Gloriana Schnurrbush screwed up her old face until it looked like a wet handkerchief in her effort to remember. It was just as well that as the years advanced her memory became increasingly selective.

Steve had in fact been a 'transit bandit'. Transit bandits were men who hung about the levator stations until they identified some acceptable prey. The bandit then squirmed his way through the waiting crowds, until he was sufficiently near the object of his transitory affections to be sure of boarding the same levator. The levator chambers were always so crowded that molestation was easy, almost unavoidable at times. The people were wedged so tightly together that movement was difficult. This restriction on mobility, combined with the high velocity between floors, meant that a transit bandit had to be a very slick operator indeed.

'My Steve was a very clever man,' Gloriana told Dab.

Steve was, in fact, the cleverest operator on Floor 87, probably the best in Aidan Beeblock, and certainly among the top half-dozen in the Fourth Sector. With ordinary luck he achieved sexual congress within the transit of nine or ten floors.

With Gloriana Schnurrbush he achieved it before they reached Floor 89.

'He was a very quick man,' she told Dab. 'Everybody admitted he was very quick.'

Gloriana soon discovered that Steve confined his operations to the levator station in vestibule 333 off corridor 18, which was where she lived. She would travel up with him, disembark, and make sure they were in the same chamber for the downward trip. Up and down they went until Steve was exhausted. Then he would go away, about midday, only to reappear the following morning with his energies restored.

After five days of this routine he recognised her.

'Bushy!' he said. 'You're bushy!'

'Wasn't that wonderful?' she asked Dab. 'He called

me Bushy even before he knew my name. A kind of telepathy or something. We were sort of made for each other.' She dabbed the corners of her eyes with arthritic fingers. 'He always called me Bushy, although Gloriana is such a nice name. Like a fairy.'

Dab put his head on one side and then on the other, as if to obtain a better focus for his big soulful eyes. Those brown eyes were saying that he knew everything, that he understood it all, but simply couldn't find the words to express what he was feeling.

'Those were the happiest days of my life,' she told him. 'Everything was perfect.' Her faded blue eyes fixed upon vacancy for a moment. 'As near perfect as anything can be.'

Perhaps Gloriana was remembering the most important particular which had caused her newfound happiness to fall some way short of perfection.

The years which Steve had spent as a transit bandit had made him impotent in bed, or in any place other than that where he had practised his specialized skills. He needed the stench and the screech of levators the way some men need exotic perfume or soft music or fishnet stockings with fancy garters. Consequently, even after Steve had moved into the module in vestibule 333, Gloriana's passionate sighs caused her to suck up the fetid air of the levator chambers, and her movements of conjunctive bliss were restrained by the contiguity of fellow passengers.

All her most intimate ecstasies continued to be strictly transitional and multi-storied.

'You see,' she explained, 'my Steve liked the feeling of going up and down.'

Dab put his head on one side and looked at her earnestly, as if to say that he could well believe it.

CHAPTER TEN

Osbert Osborne stumbled out of the sleeping-cubicle into his tiny living-room, pushed his eyelids upwards with his fingers, swayed for a few seconds in front of the autochef, and pressed the button that said *Roughage & Raisins.* He ate this farinaceous farrago where he stood and dropped the soiled dish into the disposal chute.

As he moved away his right foot failed to make direct contact with the floor, and some hostile agency kicked his legs from under him. He raised himself on one knee and looked around for the assailant.

The lacquered vase had rolled briskly away, *pinggged* against the wall, and rolled slowly back into his very hands. He scooped it up and flung it into the disposal chute.

He did the same with his supper dish, on which he discovered he'd been sitting. He came across the two empty beer cans and dealt with them in the same way. He found *Prepare Ye The Way*, and that followed. With returning memory, and some further search, he located the artificial flowers and sprigs of schiaparelli stuck to his backside with soyjoy sauce.

Ozzie glared maliciously at the blank space on the wall from which the shelf bracket had been so recently detached. The hostile agencies didn't have everything their own way. Not by any means, he told himself, as he left for the office.

Vestibule 712 off corridor 22 was jammed even more than usual by the mob besieging the levator station. Ozzie found progress impossible for the time being. He tilted his head back, in the hope that this would make it easier to breathe among the taller people who surrounded him.

The crowd swayed first this way, then that way. He was squeezed out from its centre like a pip, until he was up against the wall of the vestibule. There was a surge forward, presumably because a levator had arrived at the station and relieved some of the congestion. He was carried a little way forward along the wall, and the movement stopped again.

Someone ahead must have fallen and been hurt sufficiently badly to press a retrieval button. Within seconds the head and shoulders of a retrieval cyborg appeared above the throng. Its warning beacon occluded and flashed in synchronous alternation with a whistle that shrieked and intermitted. People fought each other to escape from the cyborg's path.

The pressure on Ozzie redoubled. He experienced a sharp pain near his left hip, and a moment afterwards a similar spasm in the region of his right kidney. He managed to twist sideways, but succeeded only in transferring the first pain from his hip to his spine, while the second pain continued unabated. He was frightened. Was this the onset of some horrible disease? Perhaps he also should crawl along next to the wall until he found a retrieval panel.

Exploration with his left hand revealed an external cause of the first affliction: the handle of a module door. Investigation with the other hand discovered the source of the second pain also: the cylinder of Meltstahl. After much elbowing and wriggling he managed to extract the offending tube from his pocket.

The crowd lurched forward after the retrieval cyborg had passed, and then swayed back again. The door handle, with deliberate malevolence, selected the lower vertebrae of Ozzie's dorsal area for especial torment. With a cry of agony he made a supreme effort and twisted round until he was facing the door. He jabbed the nozzle of the Meltstahl at the instrument of torture, and squeezed in a paroxysm of hatred.

That would bloodystop the bloodything! That would bloodystop its bloodycaper! He couldn't have squeezed the cylinder harder if he'd been intent on throttling somebody to death.

And in a way he was. This was his revenge upon an environment which, although apparently inanimate, nevertheless had the power to rise up and strike him. It was with a sense of righteous satisfaction that he grasped the door handle and felt it break off into his hand as another forward impulse in the crowded corridor moved him onwards.

Ozzie spent a typical day at Tcity Consultants: he shrank against the wall when he saw Mr Amory heading in his direction; Tentrix almost walked through him as if he wasn't there; Mustapha came into the Filing Department and abused him unmercifully for not being able to find a document which Ozzie was fairly certain he'd never received.

It wasn't until he returned home, and emptied his pockets, that he remembered the handle from the module in vestibule 712.

Ozzie held it in the palm of his hand and examined it curiously. It was shaped like a kind of hook, and you would put your hand on the upward curve of the hook to open the door. Why it should interest him, and why it should remind him of something, he couldn't guess.

He shook his head and went about his rituals: the tri-di, the autochef, the cantilevered chair. *Plip*! The tri-di projected a three-dimensional image of Princess Oriana, wet from her scallop shell, being pursued by a creature which would have looked perfectly human had it not been green and equipped with two heads. *Plop*! *Today's Surprise* was soyjoy on pumpernickel. Ozzie quietly ate his supper, and ignored the argument between the two heads as to which should enjoy the first kiss of the captured Princess. He switched off and went to bed before Coonan arrived.

The following morning he decided to take a different route to work, in the hope that it would be less congested.

Instead of turning off the main corridor into vestibule 712 he kept going. After a while he began to feel uneasy.

Never in his life had he travelled so far along corridor 22, and he'd no idea where the next levator station might be. It would be impossible to turn round and go back. Nobody, no matter how big and strong, could possibly walk against the one-way traffic flow in a city corridor.

His stomach muscles spasmed with apprehension. What if he had to keep going forwards, in a straight line, but never arriving anywhere? What if he had to keep moving until he dropped with fatigue?

But that was absurd. All he had to do was turn left or right into one of the vestibules which continued to branch off the main corridor in the usual manner. And there, coming up ahead, was a familiar sign which instructed pedestrians who wanted to use levators to get into line. He suffered the habitual pushing and kicking as he forced his way into a delevator chamber, and endured the usual nausea of its rapid descent. Nevertheless, the levator station in vestibule 704 had been less packed than vestibule 712, and he decided that he would use this route in future.

He stumbled out of the chamber at floor 64 into an unidentifiable vestibule. The one-way traffic flow snatched him up and bore him away before he was able to decipher the ceiling indicators. Waves of anxiety crashed over him. Ozzie regretted, with all the bitter sincerity in his heart, that he had deviated so far from his usual route this morning. It was unnatural and perverse. He must have been mad. How he wished he was part of the crowd struggling outside the levator station in vestibule 712! How sweetly familiar that scene had suddenly become.

Now he was lost, so completely that he had no sense of orientation. He didn't know the number of this vestibule and discovered that he'd forgotten the number of the floor. Panic seized him. He tried to recall other things and found that he couldn't: he'd forgotten the address of Tcity Consultants and the number of his own module. He didn't know where he was or where he was going, or why he should be going to any place at all. He didn't know who he was or what he was. He was a thing without memories and without hopes. He was nothing at all.

Ozzie staggered against the wall of the vestibule. The crowd had thinned out a little, and he was able to proceed at his own pace. He slithered along, supporting himself with his hands against the wall, until he came to a module door. There he stopped, rested his forehead against its smooth surface, and closed his eyes in an attempt to assemble his scrambled thoughts into some kind of pattern.

Who am I? He thought. Where am I going and what am I doing?

When he opened his eyes he saw a star shining brightly amidst a cluster of lesser stars. He blinked three or four times, which caused the lesser stars to disappear, while the star remaining at the centre took on the shape of a door handle.

He gazed at it with dazzled eyes.

There was something about the shape which gave him inconceivable pleasure. He stroked it with his hand, and his mouth became dry with excitement. This smooth shape fitted perfectly into an empty space which had been waiting for it in his imagination.

Ozzie tried to examine the door handle more dispassionately. It was shaped like a hook, but upside down, and he was struck by a curious relationship.

The handle to the door of his own module was shaped something like an elongated S or an S which had been compressed between two opposed vertical faces, with curlicues at top and bottom. The handle he was holding looked as if it had been shaped in the same way and then had its lower half removed. It was exactly like the top half of the handle on his own door, and as he tightened his fingers around its shining curve he recalled exactly the sensual memory of entering his module.

Ozzie closed his eyes. The illusion was perfect. He had come home after another meaningless day at the office.

The door opened. The familiar faceless walls of his own module greeted him. He started to go about the rituals which he now realized were so dear to him: the tri-di, the autochef, the cantilevered chair.

He opened his eyes and the destruction of the illusion brought tears to them. Again he saw the silver star which shimmered at the centre of a stellar mist. Again the silver sparklets condensed into the shape he was holding in his fist.

Now another thought struck him with the force of a revelation.

He was picturing the door handle in vestibule 712 which had tortured him so mercilessly that he'd removed it in a fit of temper. It also was like a flattened S but with its upper half removed. The handle in his fist was exactly the same as the one he had removed and taken home, except that this handle was the other way round and its long limb was raised from the door instead of lying against it. He thought of it another way: this handle and the one from vestibule 712 were component parts of the handle to his own door in corridor 22.

A strange thing started to grow in Ozzie's mind. He felt it pushing at the bony case above his ears and over his eyes. It continued to expand until he felt that the top of his head would burst.

The shape within his fingers and the shapes in his memory were parts of a harmony which was itself part of a much larger harmony. He was holding a tiny fragment of that pattern which lies at the heart of all things. The unheard song in his heart was a tiny piece of a theme in some tremendous symphony.

This door handle was a piece in some enormously complex balancing act. The pieces were so innumerable and so diverse that nobody could possibly have guessed that each self-consistent piece was necessary to the self-consistency of the whole.

Ozzie groped in his pocket, found the tube of Meltstahl, and applied it according to the instructions. Not the instructions on the tube merely; but other, mandatory instructions, which came from a place he didn't know.

CHAPTER ELEVEN

The next time Will Forstell went to the First Sector he used the traditional methods he knew so well.

After the tiresome struggling and queueing in the beeblock he came out into Thruway 5 and took the fast lane to the city centre. He cruised happily around the ringline and exited on to the south-bound paveline in Thruway 1.

The colossal dome of the Fun Palace floated past on his left like a fairy bubble of secret delights. Farther along on the right was the glittering five-pointed star which emblazoned the front of the Blue Star Club. It would have cost him a month's increments to visit places like that. The big clubs were for business managers, barbers, and others in the highest income groups.

Still, it was good to think that if he saved up his increments he would be able to visit one of these clubs some day. As it was he preferred to visit the First Sector regularly and use its less costly bars. Besides, he was still suffering from the exceptional costs of his last trip, when he had had to pay for a double journey in an auto without even . . .

He winced, and put the memory aside.

Will pushed his way amidst the throngs of pleasure-seekers. Some, like him, had come to buy whatever pleasures they could afford, but many had come merely to stare. At an open doorway, surmounted by a gaily striped canopy, he paused.

Soft music strayed out to the sidewalk and lingered in the air like an invitation. The synthesized treble of an oboe, sweetly piercing, entreated him to enter with reedy insistence. The interior was dark, but he saw the incandescent flickering as the aphrodollies at the bar flashed their credentials. While he hesitated a couple of men pushed inside ahead of him, and a fresh surge of pedestrians started to carry him away. He grabbed at the door jamb and squeezed inside.

Will could see only one aphrodolly who was unoccupied. She was sitting on a stool at the end of the bar. He stood next to her while he provided himself with a drink. As he raised the stahlex tankard to his lips someone bumped into him. He partly fell across the girl, and spilled some of his beer.

'Good evening, sir,' she said, plucking a cambric handkerchief from her sleeve.

'Sorry,' he said.

'My situation is such that I cannot remain insensible of your attention,' she said, rubbing vigorously at the beer-stained skirt with her handkerchief.

He put his tankard on the bar. 'My name's Will Forstell. What's yours?'

'I am Miss Bicknell, daughter of Charles Bicknell Esquire, a man of substance as even the most cursory of local enquiries would reveal. On my mother's side I am the grand-daughter of the Reverend Doctor Rhudde, Rector of Bergholt, where——'

'All right, all right. D'you want a drink?'

She smiled, and showed the perfect teeth that every aphrodolly possessed. 'I am indebted to you, sir, for your uncommon kindness.'

'Call me Will,' he said.

Miss Bicknell inclined her head. 'You place me even

further in your debt, my dear Mr Forstell, for your civility towards me.'

She spoke with an accent he hadn't come across before, with a pleasant burr. He noticed her hand resting on the bar as he inserted his money and punched for the drink. Her hand was slightly too large to be elegant, and it was tanned. The fingers were too strong and capable to be those of a lady, but the hand was beautifully proportioned.

Miss Bicknell took the stahlex tankard. Her face was rounded, with a curved brow, and it was almost as tanned as her hands. Her eyebrows were black and finely arched. A large bonnet was tied under her chin with a ribbon. Its flattened brim concealed her ears, but not the curls of dark hair.

'What's your scene?' he asked.

'It is called Flatford Mill.'

She raised her tankard to drink. He saw that her long sleeves were tied round with ribbons to match the one on her bonnet. A shawl was thrown around her shoulders. There was about her a certain freshness, a smell even, which had nothing to do with mere cleanliness or perfumes.

'This mill place,' he asked, 'what's it like?'

'From the window of my chamber you may, if you so wish, view the pleasantest and happiest landscape that it was ever man's good fortune to see. Indeed you should not neglect to see it. Only my natural timorousness in these matters prevents me from urging the project upon you, with more ardour than ordinary politeness would allow.'

Will, who had already made up his mind, had started nodding his acceptance after the first few words and hadn't listened to the rest. What the hell had got into these aphrodollies? A few weeks ago you didn't have to go through all this outlandish rigmarole.

They finished their beers and went out into the thruway. Miss Bicknell led the way to the first side-street and turned into it. He followed her along a small dark alleyway, through a narrow door, and into a crowded vestibule near the back of a beeblock. She unlocked her module door and drew him inside.

Will Forstell blinked.

A bright rectangle had appeared in the wall opposite. It shone with an opalescent light.

'What is it?' he asked.

'Only a window.'

He took a pace towards it, stopped, took two further hesitant paces, stopped again.

'Yes,' he agreed, doubtfully. 'But what's on the other side?'

'Pray have a look. There is no need for distress, I do assure you.'

He forced himself to move forwards until he was face to face with that dazzling light. With his nose almost pressing the glass, he looked out. What he saw immediately affected him with such a sense of unreality that he felt as if he had been transported to another planet.

'Did I not promise you something altogether splendid?' Miss Bicknell enquired.

He seized the window sill with desperate hands, to reassure himself that he had something solid to hold on to.

'What is it?' he whispered.

'Do you mean the whole scene, my dear Mr Forstell, or some particular part of it?'

He risked moving one hand from the window sill to point. 'That,' he said. 'All that up there.'

'It is that without which one of the most effectual parts of any composition would be lost. It is that element which provides the keynote, the standard of scale, and which remains the chief organ of sentiment. It is that which is the source of light and which gives value to the tones of all the other parts. In short, Mr Forstell, it is the sky.'

'Sky?'

She laughed at his incredulity, but her amusement was

pleasant and quite without any element of ridicule. Her laughter was natural and unforced, like water in a spring.

'Of course it is the sky,' she said. 'What else could it be?'

He supposed he must have known what it was the moment he looked out of the window. Even so, it was difficult to believe that what he was looking at through this window and the narrow strips which appeared between the tops of the beeblocks were parts of the same thing. Even the patch of sky outside the Autoterminus was no larger than a thumbnail compared with this.

But it wasn't merely the difference in area which was so disconcerting. The sky at which he now gazed was full of movement and colour.

Enormous white shapes sailed across this blue ocean. They appeared to be solid structures, and he examined their mountainous terrain for signs of men or other creatures. As the clouds continued on their ponderous way they slowly changed shape. Here and there they thinned out, and new fissures appeared through which the blue sky became visible. He discovered, also, that these shapes weren't entirely white. He wasn't sure whether he hadn't been sufficiently observant to begin with, or whether these tinctures of red, orange, yellow and brown had appeared with the other changes in the sky.

'If you look closely at the clouds,' said Miss Bicknell, 'you will see that there is more than one layer of them.'

Now he saw that these large masses of cloud had opaque patches moving under them. He decided that these patches were smaller clouds, floating nearer to the earth and travelling at much greater speed.

Will was used to the unvarying geometry of beeblocks and thruways with their flat surfaces and straight lines. The city horizons and skylines were always predictable. These other shapes, rounded, irregular, changing, filled him with unease.

He lowered his eyes.

In the distance were fields and woods, and nearer at hand some bushes and trees, painted with a variety of greens. A broad shadow cast by a passing cloud traversed the scene, and after its passing the colours were so fresh and bright they hurt his eyes.

'How green everything is!' he exclaimed.

Miss Bicknell laughed pleasantly. 'Not really. If you look at the cornfield over there, you will see that the part shaded by the cottage is green as you say. But over the rest of the field the corn has ripened to yellow in the sun.'

'It all looks green to me,' said Will, to whom the world had hitherto been uniformly grey.

Nearer at hand were some excessively complicated structures, also in various shades of green, which he had already guessed to be trees. How he knew this he wasn't sure, because they were quite different from the trees in the city gardens and compounds. If they were made of stahlex then that ubiquitous material had been disguised with much more than usual ingenuity.

'Those are English Elms,' she said, sensing his new focus of interest. 'They have a particular shape you can recognize, but if you're not sure you can make certain by looking at the leaves.'

'The leaves?'

'They are quite different from the leaves of any other tree and they have unequal sides.'

Will wasn't sure what she meant, but he could certainly see an infinite number of inequalities in these lopsided structures. The trunks were tall, with deeply fissured bark glimpsed at irregular intervals through the thick foliage. The lower branches were too heavy for the trees to support, and they hung downwards to a greater or lesser extent. The higher branches were more widely spreading, and just when it seemed that they might unbalance the tree, they curved upwards to form a rounded crown.

'Everything seems to be unequal,' he mumbled, thinking of the symmetry of the stahlex trees outside the Autoterminus in the Second Sector.

And yet in some strange way, beyond the reach of computation or analysis, these inequalities cancelled each other out so as to present a balance which couldn't have been achieved by the mere calculation of weights and measures. Every inconsistency was contradicted by another inconsistency, each inequality was compensated by another inequality. Every random growth was offset by another random growth, so that all the growing parts were blended into an organic whole. They were self-consistent trees in a self-consistent universe.

With wondering eyes, like a visitor from another world, he shortened his gaze again.

Down below, between grassy banks sown with purple thistles and meadow barley, spark-flecked water made its placid way. On its face the moving clouds and glittering shapes of trees mingled in shifting forms of grey and green and black, interfaced with silver shards of reflected brightness.

'And what's that?' he asked.

'A river.'

'River?'

He repeated the word mechanically, as he had done when she first mentioned the sky and leaves. They were words he knew, from stories on the tri-di and from their use in metaphor. It was vastly different actually to see the things which the words represented. Like the water-fowl, for instance, to which Miss Bicknell next drew his attention.

They were playing on the surface of the river. A moorhen flirted white tail coverts, and repeatedly nodded its red forehead as it pursued a bobbing course along the bank. Something had disturbed a coot, which pattered along the water until, with legs trailing behind, it raised its body from the surface in heavy, laboured flight. A pair of mallard ducks were dabbling together where willows stooped their branches to the water. The drake kept bowing its green head at the female again and again, in an ecstasy of courtship, so that the sunlight kept glossing his neck with a dazzle of purple.

Will soon lost interest in these creatures, despite their unfamiliarity. His attention strayed and, like driftwood, followed the slowly moving water until it was arrested by some wooden gates.

The heavy double gates were blackened by water and time. The bricked enclosure was filled with water, so that the pressure on the other side held the swinging gates firmly together, although some imperfection in their joining caused a spout of water to escape. Another trickle of water showed that a side culvert wasn't fully closed.

Miss Bicknell moved away from him, made an adjustment to a control somewhere in the darkened room, and returned to his side.

The noises of running waters reached his ears. It was the noise of water from the gap between the lock gates and from the culvert; and the noise of water lapping against old masonry, and rippling against the trailing willows, and bubbling in the reed thickets where the nests were, and swirling round a slimy post for tethering river craft, and scrabbling over the rotten planks of a derelict barge, and gurgling around the water plants, and squabbling over permanently wet stones beneath which the loaches dozed.

Intermingled with these water noises Will also heard, for the first time in his life, a coot loudly clearing its throat and the soft croaking of moorhens.

He pointed again. 'What's that?'

'It's a lock,' she replied. 'It was used for moving boats from one level to another.'

'Why would anybody want to do that?'

'It was a most expeditious method of transferring merchandise from the place of manufacture to distant markets. Indeed, it is accepted beyond a peradventure that it was the work of the indefatigable Mr Richard Brindley that ushered in the First Industrial Revolution.'

Will continued to stare at that tranquil scene

The lock was at the heart of all those water noises, and its wet black wood reflected the light of the omnipresent sky as brightly as if it were draped with snow. It seemed to be as old as the ancient elms, and to be as natural a part of this scene as the moving clouds, the stooping willows and the softly sliding water.

New thoughts came to Will Forstell, but so vague that he couldn't possibly have tried to formulate them. So lost was he that he couldn't have said whether Miss Bicknell's commentary was putting some of his thoughts into words or not.

'On each swing door,' she was saying, 'is a rack and pinion for raising and lowering the sluice. This engineering device was used on lock gates two centuries before it became a standard feature in the steering mechanism of autos. The lock——'

'Don't talk about autos!' he interrupted.

'The lock was the most advanced piece of engineering in its day, and the greatest spur to business enterprise. But it is as harmonious a part of this picture as the courting mallards or the ripening corn. The hand of man and the hand of nature seem to be occupied with the same task.'

'I don't know what you're talking about,' he said. 'I don't understand what it's all about.'

Miss Bicknell spoke quietly. 'There's nothing to understand. It isn't about anything.'

As Will continued to look through the window, the feelings of unease which had afflicted him at the first view now mounted to a level of intensity which made him want to be sick. The moving clouds and the sliding river made him long for the massive solidity of the bee-blocks. The noise of water and the cries of birds made him yearn for the tramping feet and whistling cyborgs in the city corridors. Those vivid greens made his eyes ache for the restful grey of the endless perspectives in the thruways.

He swallowed hard, and turned away from the window. 'I've had enough,' he said. 'Switch it off.'

Miss Bicknell moved away from him, and there was a scarcely audible click. The screen opaqued, and the landscape disappeared. A recorded voice began to speak.

'This scenario represented a scene on the River Stour as seen from a window in Flatford Mill. Constable said "I associate my 'careless boyhood' with all that lies on the banks of the Stour; those scenes made me a painter and I am grateful."'

Will's hands groped in the darkness, and found the plump arms of the Reverend Doctor Rhudde's granddaughter. She laughed softly and allowed herself to be captured.

'Although Constable is thought of as a painter of Nature, every object in his paintings shows the intervention of man for economic purposes. The trees are cut back from the fields, the land is efficiently ploughed, hedges and fences prevent the cattle from straying, the river is canalized. Only the sky is unaffected by business enterprise ...'

His hand found the ribbon under her dimpled chin. He pulled and the bonnet came away from her head. The dark curls tumbled around his fingers.

'For the skyscape we synthesized a film from the cloud studies which Constable made during his summer trips to Hampstead. He annotated them with date, time of day, direction of wind ...'

His mouth travelled down the curved brow towards her nose.

'Can't you switch it off?' he grumbled.

'No. It's part of the contract, but you needn't listen.'

'Exotic Scenarios Corporation hopes that you will enjoy your stay in Flatford Mill, and that you will come again, and . . .'

He wasn't listening.

Miss Bicknell took his hand and led him across the room to a low bed which smelled sweetly of fresh cut hay.

CHAPTER TWELVE

Taggart stared at the featureless stahlex ceiling of his sleeping-cubicle, and listened to the dead voices echoing in his memory.

'He's in the way,' said the harsh voice of his father.

His mother protested softly. 'I'm sure he isn't. He spends most of his time in his own room, watching the children's educational programmes and learning——'

'He'd learn much better at the sector crèche. That's where we would have sent him at the very beginning, if you hadn't this silly, sentimental attachment to him.'

'But I loved him even before he was born! Can't you understand that?'

'No. I can't. All I can understand is that he's in the way, and that he'll be out of the way when we send him to the sector crèche.'

'But you can't say we're overcrowded. You hardly see him except at meal times, and if the three of us——'

'Four of us,' interrupted the rasping voice.

There was a silence. The small boy, who had been listening in horror to this argument about his destiny, strained his ears to catch his mother's response. Her voice had been growing fainter with each exchange, and he feared that next time he wouldn't be able to hear it at all.

'Yes,' she murmured, 'sometimes there are four of us.'

'There will be four of us this afternoon!' his father shouted. 'Or there will be if that boy is here. And if he is here he'll be in the way.'

Taggart slipped out of the module early in the afternoon, and lost himself in the faceless crowd of the bee-block. It was good to be one of those anonymous faces. He drifted round the endless corridors and vestibules like a microbe in a diseased and sluggish bloodstream.

He was terrified at the thought of being sent to the crèche in the First Sector, where robotic devices of various kinds looked after children from birth to adolescence. Many were the frightening stories that were told about it. If only half the stories were only half true, he knew that he would go mad if he were sent there. He was even more terrified of being deprived of his mother. Life without her was as unimaginable as life without light, or air, or food. It was only the knowledge of her steadfast love for him, and of her opposition to his father at least in this respect, that kept his small feet plodding around the endless corridors and vestibules; and it was that knowledge which finally drove them back to the module in the evening.

The module was silent.

He crossed the empty living-area and listened outside the cubicle where his parents slept. All was silence. Slowly he opened the door and entered upon his apocalypse.

His mother was alone and asleep. She was lying face downwards, with her arms above her head. Her face was turned sideways and it was wet, perhaps with a mixture of sweat and tears. The curls of fair hair above her ears were damp, and stuck to her temple above a light blue vein which visibly throbbed.

Her back was bare. The sheets had been pushed down to below her waist, presumably because she couldn't tolerate anything which could chafe upon her flesh.

Taggart opened his mouth to cry out, but his horror and astonishment were so great that no sound came. He didn't understand. Even when he had grown to be a man, he would understand it as little as the small boy who, with his mouth still open to cry, backed out of his mother's room.

That night it was very quiet. His father returned, but the other woman didn't come with him. Taggart lay awake, his eyes wide and unblinking in the darkness.

Until now his young life had possessed some kind of pattern in a self-consistent order of things. He had known where things were, and what they were used for, and what they meant. If he didn't know where something was he knew where to look for it, because it was part of a general pattern in which he too had his place. And if he couldn't find what he was looking for he had only to ask; he had only to name it or describe it and his mother would find it for him. Things were used for self-evident purposes. They had natural functions in the general pattern. If he didn't know what things meant he had only to ask. His mother always knew the answer even when she wouldn't tell him.

'That is something you'll understand when you're older,' she said.

He had always believed her.

Now everything had changed. Something terribly different had happened which altered everything else. He no longer knew where things were, nor what they were used for, nor what they meant. He knew instinctively that he couldn't ask his mother about it. He was certain that she didn't know the answer herself.

The next night the noises returned.

He heard the droning monotone of the other woman, and the harsh voice of his father. The other sounds now had the power to make pictures appear in his mind, and he leaped from his cot in anguish.

Taggart rushed at the door which connected his sleeping-cubicle with the living-area, but it was locked. He kicked it frantically.

'Stop it!' he screamed. 'Stop it! Stop it!'

The sounds stopped.

'Momma!' he cried. 'Momma!'

The door opened.

His father's rickety figure jerked in the frame like a badly handled puppet. The long dog face and the brown dog eyes looked at him in bewilderment, as if unable to recall who he was. Behind his father, lying on a folding day bed, he saw the other woman for the first time. She wasn't wearing a wig, and her head looked wet and shiny. After staring at him for a moment she turned her naked back, and the prominence of her deltoids made her shoulders look like those of a well-built man.

Taggart returned his attention to his father's face, where the expression of bewilderment had turned to one of fury.

'What d'you want?' he shouted.

'I want my momma.'

'She's not here.'

'She is, dad. I heard her crying.'

'I've just told you. She's not here.'

Taggart knew she must be in the room somewhere, although she was outside his line of sight. She must be close up against the wall, to either the right or the left of the door.

'Dad, dad,' he begged, 'what are you doing to her? What's the matter with you? I can't understand anything.'

His father lowered himself briefly on to the ball of his left foot, repositioned his right foot and braced himself for action. It was now that Taggart saw he was holding something in his big right hand. As his father raised it above his head, Taggart saw that it was a whip. The handle was black and shiny, and the thong was woven out of stahlex thread.

'Don't! Please don't!'

It was his mother's voice, but it sounded strange, almost as if she were trying to speak and eat something at the same time. Her voice was soft, as always, but there was an urgency in it, a kind of desperate authority, which Taggart hadn't heard before.

'Don't! Please don't! Not against our boy!'

Taggart expected his mother to come across and intercede between himself and that upraised whip. She didn't. He could locate her, however, because her voice came from the right. This was confirmed by the other woman, who turned her head to glance in that direction, apparently amused by the earnestness of his mother's plea.

'Momma!' he called. 'Are you all right?'

'I told you he was in the way,' his father yelled. 'Didn't I tell you he was in the way? He's just proved it.'

Taggart stepped forward. His father's thin arm jumped higher, and when he jerked his big hand the whip uncurled. Taggart recognized the sound it made. He'd heard it often enough. The stahlex thong bit into his back and fled again like a snake.

He fell backwards with a cry, and the door closed.

At first he thought he couldn't live with the pain. He scratched his arms and thighs until they bled, hoping that these other wounds might somehow divert some of the pain from his back. He cried and walked up and down in his sleeping-cubicle, and eventually the sharpness disappeared from the agony and it became a dull ache. He found that he could bear to lie sideways in his cot.

Some while after that the wounded flesh on his back developed a warm feeling, and in that warmth it seemed to him that he was joined to his mother in a love more intimate than ever before.

CHAPTER THIRTEEN

Sylvia was trying to relax in the unaccommodating chair.

'No, I'm not!' Mr Felixtowe was shouting into the telephone, eyes closed. 'What you don't seem to realize is that I'm doing you a favour, Mr Smythe.'

Sylvia listened to the angry voice, and brooded about the success of the Work Project.

In prehistorical times, and in the first few thousand years of recorded time, this problem had quite simply not existed. *Homo abilis* had lived like a bird, with most of his mental and physical energies devoted to discovering and devouring the next mouthful of food. When darkness fell he crawled into his cave, his adobe hut or skin tent, and made his nightly rediscovery of happiness in human warmth. In the morning the sun rose, and he rose with it to resume the endless struggle to prolong the lives of himself and his loved ones.

'Let me put it another way,' yelled Mr Felixtowe into the telephone. 'Let me put it as simply as I can, in the hope that even you will be able to understand.'

After the unchanging centuries of living at subsistence level there had been innovations, gradual and unnoticed at first, but then proceeding at an increasing rate until the whole nature of life was transformed.

Homo sapiens began to specialize in order to exploit his individual skills and the potentialities of his local environment; trade made it possible to share out the benefits of specific skills and geographical areas. He began to enjoy something more than the simple necessities of life, and of these new pleasures one of the most important was leisure. Money was invented so that the fruits of one skill or area could be more readily exchanged for the fruits of another. Economic activity became so complex that a man could no longer identify what his own labours contributed to the welfare of himself, his family, or the community.

But then mechanization and automation brought the millennium within sight. Individual toil had lost its manifest purpose, but this didn't seem to matter. All problems would be solved because men wouldn't need to work. Work, which had begun to appear meaningless, truly would be meaningless because it wouldn't exist.

'You have no stocks, Mr Smythe,' continued the testy voice of Mr Felixtowe, 'owing to the inefficient way in which you manage, or mismanage, Depot Number Five. At the same time your fool of a sales manager has committed you to supply considerable quantities in the next couple of days. Just to make the problem completely insuperable, you now discover that the Stahlex Corporation can't deliver fresh supplies to you for over a week.' Mr Felixtowe's voice thickened and became rich with satisfaction. 'You are in serious trouble, Mr Smythe, and there doesn't appear to be any solution.'

Mechanization and automation, however, had not provided the solution. The rate of change became too swift for men to adapt to it. To the astonishment of the privileged minority, the increasingly wealthy labour force became increasingly discontented with its way of life. A deep and unrecognized frustration showed itself in acts of violence which were apparently without motive. People in positions of executive authority became more and more incompetent to direct the operations for which they were made responsible. The labour force, or what had once been a labour force, was beyond control. Business enterprises had grown so large that they too were beyond the control of the directors who were nominally running them for millions of apathetic shareholders. What economists used to mean by 'surplus', and what accountants used to mean by 'profit', ceased to have any real significance.

And still the nations of the world and the big multinational companies continued to compete with each other for the planet's dwindling stocks of raw materials and sources of energy. The human species was in serious trouble, and there didn't seem to be any solution.

'But there is a solution,' Mr Felixtowe said, in a resonant, statesman-like voice. 'It's our policy always to carry a stock of all the more popular products. Consequently we are carrying a stock of the items you require so desperately.'

But there was a solution. Genetic engineering had produced a race of men and women whose superior congenital endowment could be further enhanced by brain surgery. The Executives were virtually a different species: *Homo sapientior*. They had taken over the managerial problems of the planet as a matter of course.

'Purely to help you out of an unpleasant situation, Mr Smythe, a situation of your own making, I am willing to let you have some of our stock. It will leave us in a weak position on this product, but I want to help you. And who knows, I might want to ask you for a favour sometime?'

Mr Felixtowe, eyes closed, grinned without mirth in Sylvia's direction.

The Executives ran everything. They managed the colossal automated factories; and they managed the colossal automated cities. All the Chief Executives, whether they had business or civic responsibilities, were responsible to the Central Executive. For the first time in the history of the planet all executive responsibilities, of whatever nature, were in the hands of a supremely intelligent, educated and rational élite.

Mr Felixtowe named a price. Sylvia, although the main trend of her thoughts was elsewhere, and although she was unused to thinking in the monetary terms of the cities, was astounded by the figure.

'You tell me now, Yes or No!' shouted Mr Felixtowe, rising to his feet in a passion and almost dropping the telephone receiver. 'Yes or No, d'you hear me, Smythe? If you say No it'll be a great relief to me, I can tell you, because my staff here will think I've taken leave of my senses in giving you all our stock.'

The Citizens, who comprised over ninety-nine per cent of the population, were confined with few exceptions to the enclosed cities. The exceptions were those who exercised skills which it had so far proved impossible to mechanize or automate, and which couldn't be exploited within the cities. There were, for example, the colonies on the other side of the Minch, where crofters wove their tweeds by hand on single-width looms. Sylvia guessed that Jan, much as he prized his jacket, would have thought first of the French peasants. In September they still took their weekly walk through the Sauternes vineyards, picking only those grapes which had been shrivelled by *pourriture noble*; and their German counterparts still used the traditional methods of collecting grapes for the *Trockenbeerenauslese* wines of the Rheingau.

Mr Felixtowe was clutching his chest, and seemed to be on the verge of a paroxysm. 'Don't you try to bargain with me!' he screamed. 'I'll not have it! You pay my price and I'll help you. That's fair enough, isn't it? Just say Yes or No and don't try to argue. I'll not have it, Smythe. D'you hear me? I'll not have it!'

The Central Executive had devised a varied programme for improving the quality of life in the cities. The most important part of this programme was the Work Project, which had re-introduced labour-intensive economic activities based upon the distribution of cheap stahlex products.

Sylvia looked at the big stahlex desk, treated to simulate mahogany with a tooled leather top; she looked at the walls, unfitted with mirrors to show that there wasn't any need to create an illusion of space; she looked at Felixtowe's face, with its gorged veins, closed eyes and tightly working mouth; she listened to the whirling words, now domineering and now wheedling, now demanding and now cajoling.

This was what they had created; or re-created. An

early twentieth-century novelist had called it 'a world of telegrams and anger'.

'All right, Greg,' said Mr Felixtowe, changing to the Christian name as if to reward the man he'd just beaten. 'I'm glad you've decided to be sensible, although I don't know what my people will say. Perhaps I can ask you for a favour sometime.' He replaced the receiver, sat down, and grinned at her again. 'Just an internal call,' he said, 'and then we can finish our discussion.'

'Go ahead,' she agreed.

Mr Felixtowe dialled. 'Is that Taggart? Well listen to me, idiot. D'you remember all that junk stock you over-purchased last month? Yes, I should hope you don't forget it. I certainly won't. Well I've just sold all of it – *all* of it, d'you hear? – at an unbelievable price. Get it all sent off to Depot Number Five before that fool Greg Smythe realizes that he's been an even bigger fool than he normally is.'

Mr Felixtowe concluded his instructions to Taggart, sat back, and extracted a heavy pair of spectacles without lenses. As he pushed the spectacles up his nose his eyes opened and stared at Sylvia without blinking.

'I'm sorry for that interruption to our talk,' he said, but she could tell from the tone of his voice that he'd been glad to give a practical illustration.

'Not at all,' she said. 'I found the interlude very instructive.'

'Good, good. Have you any more questions?'

'Yes.' She put the question entirely in the manner of an academic query, without any hint of criticism. 'Why did you trick that man into paying more than he need have done for stock you didn't want anyway?'

'It's good business.'

'I'm not sure what you mean.'

Mr Felixtowe's naked eyes began to water. Her own eyes began to water in sympathy, and she was glad when he removed the spectacles so that his eyelids could drop their protective shields.

'It increases our profits,' he said, blindly. 'That's all there is to it.'

Sylvia couldn't entirely suppress her astonishment. She hadn't dreamed that this sort of thing might start to happen. 'But why should you want to do that? It won't make any difference to your personal income. You'll receive no more than the state annuity plus the increment for the job.'

'I know that. But it keeps Depot Number One at the top of the table.'

She began to feel that she'd lost all control over the direction which the dialogue was taking. 'The table?'

'I arranged with Tcity Consultants for the accounts of the various depots to be audited every month, and the results published in a profitability table. Depot Number One has been at the top of that table ever since we started.'

'You don't care how you win, so long as you win?'

Mr Felixtowe put his spectacles back on, and the magnets in the heavy frames pulled at the magnetic strips sewn into his atrophied eyelids. His eyes clicked open and stared into her face. Sylvia observed his forehead, which projected before hollowing in its descent to the sharp eye-bones. She recalled Lavater's admission that *'Foreheads of this kind deceived me more than any other, when I first began to observe.'* The Swiss physiognomist had *'supposed them penetrating, and they were only crafty'*.

'Madame,' he said. 'There is no sentiment in business.'

This ancient piece of proverbial wisdom, unused for so many years, startled her at first; but then it seemed as inevitable as a rhyming couplet closing the scene in an Elizabethan comedy. Her Executive memory presented her with dozens of historical businessmen from the nineteenth and twentieth centuries. The 'businessman' had begun to disappear early in the twenty-first century, although he lingered on as a type in contemporary fiction for some time after that: fictional businessmen had always reflected business lifestyles which were defunct at the time of writing.

'Are you happy in your work, Mr Felixtowe?'

He opened a lower side drawer in his desk, immediately found what he wanted, and handed it across to her.

She examined the circular object placed in her hand. In the middle there was a picture of a blacksmith clasping the hand of a miner. In front of them was a figure of Justice, holding a pair of scales. The entire scene was encircled by the words *Workingmen of every country unite together to defend your rights.*

'I found it in a curio shop,' he said, 'in one of the sidestreets off Thruway 1.'

'It's a fine piece of work.'

'And probably very old,' he added.

Sylvia turned it over and looked at the dial and pointers of a watch. Over three hundred years old, she decided, and probably sold for a few shillings at the time of the First International in London. The metal around the face was embossed with the words *We require eight hours for work, eight hours for our instruction and eight hours for repose.*

'The motto on the front of that watch states a great truth,' he said, and only now did he answer her question. 'Yes. I am happy in my work. I consider that all Citizens lucky enough to have been selected owe a debt of gratitude to the Central Executive for introducing the Work Project.'

She handed the watch back to him. The irony of that ancient demand for shorter working hours constricted her throat, and she didn't speak.

Mr Felixtowe replaced the watch and closed the drawer. His eyes had filled with water again. He removed his spectacles and put them in a slit pocket. His swollen eyelids closed, squeezing out two heavy tears which followed a jerky course down his cheeks.

Sylvia stood up. 'Now I think I should like to see Mr Taggart.'

He reached for the telephone.

CHAPTER FOURTEEN

Osbert Osborne awoke two hours earlier than was usual for him, and was soon convinced that some species of half-suppressed excitement would prevent him from falling asleep again.

He arose, performed his morning rituals, scoffed his Roughage & Raisins, and set off. There was sufficient time in hand for him to take a roundabout route, and risk being lost for a long time, before heading directly for the office. So he passed the indicators to his usual levator station in vestibule 712, and also to the newly discovered station in vestibule 704. He kept going until increasing apprehension made him turn left into vestibule 639, where he was forced to turn left again into corridor 23. He pursued this backward course until he was directed by ceiling indicators to a levator station in vestibule 662. In this vestibule his darting eyes discovered that the door handles were in the form of knobs.

The Meltstahl performed with its usual efficacy, and he slipped the doorknob into his pocket.

At the office, all day, he was aware of it nestling there. Its weight and structure seemed to testify to things he could only guess at. It ceased to have any association with door handles: it was a magic orb; a new planet; the eye of a god; the breast of a goddess; a sphere in which the inaudible music of the universe was crystallized.

Mustapha, hot from Market Research, swept into the Filing Department and started to shout before he was fully through the door.

'I want the file on depot turnover showing the breakdown by sales to each market sector.'

Ozzie picked up a file from the tray. 'You've come to the wrong place.'

'What d'you mean?' Mustapha's astonishment was so great that he almost tripped over his own feet. 'What the hell d'you mean by that remark? This is the Filing Department, isn't it?' Mustapha put his hands on his hips, and gazed around the tabulated shelves with an air of contemptuous enquiry. 'Or perhaps I am mistaken.'

Ozzie carefully slotted the file into its place, and reached for another from the tray. 'You're not mistaken, Mustapha. As it happens, this is the Filing Department.'

'Well then!' Mustapha's temper started to get out of control. 'I've said I want that file on depot turnover, and I want it now and not tomorrow!'

Ozzie slotted the next file into place. 'You're wasting your time here, I'm afraid.'

'What d'you mean? I want——'

'Let's not go through that again, Mustapha. I gave you the file you are enquiring about two days ago, and you haven't yet returned it. So I'd suggest you investigate the chaos in your own department before you trouble me again.'

Mustapha opened his mouth, and his jaws half closed several times as if to expel some partially formed but inaudible syllable. His face turned pink, then deep red, and abruptly a ghastly white. Finally he turned round and went out of the Filing Department as if intending to slam the door, although for some reason he closed it quietly.

Ozzie discovered that he was trembling. When he held his hand before his face he could see his fingers jumping.

An acid distillation curdled the juices in his stomach, and he staggered against a filing cabinet. He felt very ill. If he could have stiffened the sinews in his legs and made them move, he would have run after Mustapha to apologize. He would have liked to catch Mustapha before he reached the Market Research Department so that he wouldn't have to make his apologies in front of Tentrix and a roomful of other grinning people.

'Mustapha!' he would say. 'Mustapha! I'm terribly sorry I spoke to you like that. I don't know what came over me. Forgive me, Mustapha. A man in your position must have a lot on his mind. It's no wonder that you forget having taken a file from time to time. Anyway, I should have come and collected it. It's all my fault, Mustapha, and I hope . . .'

The imaginary voice was still prattling away inside Ozzie's head when the door opened and Tentrix came in. It was unusual for her to come into the Filing Department at any time. Far from asking her what she wanted, Ozzie ignored her completely. She poked at a few files in an uncertain manner, hovered for a moment, and finally went away empty-handed. Just before she closed the door he fancied that she had cast a backward glance in his direction. He was so surprised that his head jerked involuntarily to look at her. But the door had closed.

The idea of Tentrix noticing him was so astounding that he quite forgot his desire to prostrate himself before Mustapha and crave his forgiveness. Ozzie straightened up. An unaccustomed warmth bathed his stomach, and slowly spread upwards to suffuse his lungs and irradiate his throat and face. He was filled up, like a bottle under a tap, with an unwonted sensation of well-being.

The exaltation faded, but not completely. A pleasant afterglow made his nerves tingle with a new awareness of being in a living body. This vital warmth was renewed when he returned home and took the doorknob from his pocket. The doorknob was the first thing he thought of when he awoke the following morning.

How did this begin? he wondered, as he tapped the stud on the autochef. What had started him on this new life?

And then he remembered.

It was when he had missed his turning on the way home from the office, and had clung to a door handle for support in an unknown vestibule. How long ago was that? It seemed like months, even years, but it could have been little more than a week.

He saw the door handle again in his imagination. It was a shining star, surrounded by silver mists and rainbow colours. Again he extended his fingers into the sparkling nimbus and identified the shape of a ring in his hand. As Ozzie ate his Roughage & Raisins he was overtaken by a different hunger, sharp and insistent. He knew he could satisfy it only by finding the object that had transformed his life.

He began the quest that very morning, by setting out for the office along vestibule 710 and returning home by vestibule 711. The next day he went via vestibule 708 and came back through 709, and moved the scene of his operations daily in this manner so as to cover the ground thoroughly. He continued without success in the prime objective of the quest, although, coming home on the fourth day in vestibule 705, he picked up a long, fluted handle, which he liked so much he could scarcely bear to put it down.

Each morning he turned off corridor 22 at a different point, and pursued his course down the vestibules like a ravening tiger, with eyes switching from side to side in search of quarry. The mystic ring continued to elude him, but whenever his eye detected a new shape his heart would beat with such violence that his breath was caught in his windpipe. When he reached the office without having made any addition to his collection, as was usually the case, he was all the more eager to try a new route on the way home.

After a very short while Ozzie lost track of his previous excursions, which tended to meander about somewhat despite his attempt to impose a pattern on them. He found himself traversing sections of corridors and vestibules which he couldn't remember, but which he suspected he might have travelled along half-a-dozen times.

The thing to do was keep records of where he'd been. He took a piece of paper, wrote *Corridor 22* at the top of it, and underlined the heading. No sooner was this done than he decided the caption wasn't sufficiently grand. He threw the paper away, took a fresh piece, and slowly and carefully printed CORRIDOR XXII at the head of it. It wasn't until he sat back to admire the effect that he realized he'd placed it too far to the left. So he . . .

Finally he was satisfied. Under the printed heading there was a second heading which read *Vestibules Explored As Far As Corridor 20*. Under this there was a sub-heading on each side of the page: *Even Numbers* on the left and *Odd Numbers* on the right. Under these he listed the numbers of the vestibules he was certain he had explored: 712 to 668 on the left and 711 to 667 on the right.

That done, he sat back and contemplated his handiwork with enormous satisfaction.

He wondered what the source of this satisfaction could be. Perhaps it was simply the pleasure of seeing his recent activities so neatly tabulated; or perhaps he enjoyed seeing evidence of the progress of his quest, because the listed vestibules at least showed where the ring was not to be found; or it might be something altogether more difficult to grasp. Perhaps these digits showed that his life was beginning to develop some kind of a pattern? Ozzie shook his head and went to bed.

The next day he pushed back the frontiers of his ignorance a little further, by travelling along vestibules farther up the numerical scale: 714 on the way to the office, and 713 on the way home. He added these numbers to the two columns which listed the extent of his explorations, and was abruptly overwhelmed by a voracious impatience. Saliva sprang into his mouth, and dribbled from his bottom lip.

With anticipatory fingers he added to his columnar records the numbers of the next vestibules he intended to explore – 716 and 715 – and immediately rushed out of the module to do just that. He traversed vestibule 716 as far as corridor 20, and returned by 715 where he was immediately rewarded by a rectangular handle with bevelled edges.

In the days to come he visited not only additional vestibules, which ran from corridor 22 across corridor 21 to corridor 20, but also additional corridors and floors on which he knew he'd never set foot before. For long periods the quest for the ring was forgotten in the excitement of covering new territory and adding to his growing collection.

He dreamed of leaving Aidan Beeblock, of crossing Thruway 4 and exploring Cuthbert Beeblock on the other side. The world was his oyster, with the continuous promise of hidden pearls inside its lip. He lived in an expanding universe, where a myriad corridors beckoned to him like stars.

As his forays became more wide-ranging he had to start new sheets to record the additional corridors and floors. He remembered, also, that his original scheme of notation had made no provision for his distant sortie from corridor 22 – was it through vestibule 639? – when he had collected his third handle on his return through vestibule 662. It was a doorknob, actually, rather than a handle. He was certain of the second vestibule number because it was inscribed on the label which he attached to every piece in his collection.

The columns of vestibule numbers under their corridor

headings became increasingly straggling and untidy, and they seemed unworthy of the enterprise they were supposed to reflect.

Detailed maps would be better, he decided.

CHAPTER FIFTEEN

After five minutes Taggart was still on the telephone, and the conversation showed few signs of reaching a conclusion.

Sylvia squirmed around on the hard seat of her chair, and discovered that by dangling first one arm and then the other over its inflexible back, she could give exquisite relief to the pains in her side. She could devise no remedy for the recurrent cramp behind her knees. As soon as she returned to Lindisfarne she was going to recommend to the Central Executive that their ergonomists looked at office furniture in the cities as a matter of urgency.

The office was very small.

Her knees were pressing against Taggart's stahlex desk, and her hamstrings were almost screaming to be allowed to stretch. The unyielding pressure of the chair against her back, and the knowledge that the chair itself was pressed hard against the wall behind, made her want to jump to her feet and shout that people couldn't possibly work under conditions as constricted as this.

But people obviously did.

'I'm sorry you've been so inconvenienced,' Taggart was saying to the telephone in a conciliatory voice, 'but if you could——'

He was interrupted by a flow of abuse from the other end of the line.

'If you could give me the consignment number,' he resumed equably, 'I'd be able to trace the goods immediately. You'll find the consignment number at the top of——'

More violent abuse intervened.

Sylvia tried to forget her pains by making a closer scrutiny of things outside herself.

The most interesting object for observation was Taggart's face. She saw how incessant worrying had cut parallel fissures across his forehead, and worn deep grooves into the sides of his jowl. The flesh around his eyes was blue and shiny, as if from lack of sleep, but the eyes themselves sparkled with almost unnatural vivacity beneath horizontal eyebrows. She looked at the stahlex wall behind Taggart's chair, which had been polished to a mirror finish in the usual city manner to give an illusion of space. She watched a hundred heads nodding in unison as Taggart conceded some point being made by the vituperative caller.

Taggart, during the course of this telephone conversation, kept scrabbling amongst the disorderly heaps of papers on his desk. From time to time he fished out a letter or a memorandum, presumably in the hope that it might have some bearing upon the matter under dispute; but after a brief scrutiny he always discarded such documents and started rummaging about once more. At one point he jotted down a column of figures on a scribble pad, added them from bottom to top, then top to bottom and ticked the total.

Sylvia felt somewhat as she might have done if she'd been privileged to observe palaeolithic men eating meat before they had learned how to use fire; or to watch the Mayas building their temples on the tops of pyramids without inventing the wheel; or to hear a Greek poet singing dactylic verses in praise of old wine before the discovery of cork.

This was how it must have been before the development

of management science. This was the way managers must have behaved before the development of the Executive class.

Taggart, after much nodding of his head towards his invisible tormentor, and repeated promises to look into the matter, was finally able to bring the conversation to an end. He replaced the receiver on its handset, where it rang again immediately. Without having removed his hand from the instrument he returned the receiver to his ear, and was promptly immersed in another argument.

Once again he was apologizing, maintaining perfect self-control, attempting explanations which were interrupted, and poking around among the shambles on his desk in the hope that something might turn up to clarify the issues involved.

Sylvia watched the repeat performance with growing respect for the protagonist, accompanied by an odd sense that it couldn't really be happening.

Here was a man of only average intelligence, or whose IQ at best would lie somewhere in the upper quartile of the normal curve for natural intelligence. He represented an organization which was no more than a rag-bag of clerical systems which bore a fairly remote relationship to an ill-organized series of manual operations; all the activities were continuously subject to malfunction, human error, bad judgment, temperamental bias and simple ignorance. Yet this man was connected by telephone to all potential customers in Tcity, any of whom could ring him at their own convenience and ask questions about the availability, prices and so on, of a wide range of goods.

The only aids Taggart had were the advice of colleagues, if he could locate them on the internal telephone; his memory, which was selective and imperfect besides; a mass of ill-assorted papers containing data which was inaccurate when it was produced, and became increasingly inaccurate with every minute that passed; and an entity more dubious than any of these, which he thought of as his intuition.

'Early next week,' Taggart was informing a caller. 'Yes. By Tuesday afternoon at the very latest.'

Sylvia gasped. On the basis of a very limited number of facts this man was actually trying to predict the future! And although he had so little control over it, he was binding himself by promises about what it would contain! It was crazy, and yet this was how they must have worked. She watched his face, glistening with sweat, with the lines of stress across the forehead and around the mouth. She noticed his horizontal eyebrows again, and recalled the thirty-fifth physiognomical rule of Lavater, which stated that '*Horizontal eyebrows, rich and clear, always denote understanding, coldness of heart, and capacity for framing plans.*'

It went without saying that any Executive carried immeasurably more responsibility than even the most senior manager in any city organization. But as normal intellectual endowment, combined with the automatic nature of their management support systems, enabled any Executive to clear a standard day's work in an hour or so. Moreover, Executives never worried about the decisions they made because they knew they were always right. This wasn't a matter of conceit or arrogance. Executives always made the right decisions because they were applying enhanced intelligence to data which was fed to them from the totally integrated information contained in the cybernet.

Taggart was doing a much more difficult job than any Executive!

The next time he returned the telephone receiver to its rest it didn't ring. The silence was unnatural. She saw him glance at a quartz crystal clock set into the mirrored wall. The light-emitting diodes indicated the start of the two-hour lunch break. Surely that couldn't be an expression of regret on Taggart's strained features?

'Mr Felixtowe said you wanted to talk to me.' It was a flat statement in a flat voice, very unlike the tonal variations he'd used in speaking to people on the telephone.

She leaned forward in the uncomfortable chair, glad to have an excuse for making such an exaggerated movement. 'I was hoping we might have a little chat. Perhaps in view of the time we could do it over a drink and something to eat?'

He didn't respond.

'There must be a saloon in the thruway?'

'I suppose so. I always go to a bar in one of the side-streets.'

Taggart opened the top drawer of his desk and began sweeping everything into it. As the letters and papers hadn't been in any order before, it presumably didn't matter if they were jumbled up again.

'It's difficult to talk to me during working hours,' he said, and smiled in a way that she thought had something of self-satisfaction in it. 'Unless you can get me on the phone, of course.'

She laughed whole-heartedly, to show that she appreciated the joke.

Taggart had now cleared everything from the top of his desk. He closed the drawer and stood up. His next actions caused her some concern.

First he stood on tiptoe, extended his arms as far as he could above his head, until his body grew as stiff and straight as if it were being drawn upon a rack. He appeared to stretch, under the force of some invisible and diabolic machine which was prising his vertebrae apart and opening gaps between his joints. His figure assumed the elongation of an El Greco saint.

He screwed up his eyes until they looked as if they'd been stitched, and opened his mouth as wide as it would go. The yawn was so extensive that extra flesh had to be mobilized to serve the ligatures at the sides of his mouth. These reserves of skin were pulled down from his cranium, and stretched so tightly across his face that it seemed a matter of luck whether the sharp ridges of his eyebrows or of his cheekbones would be first to pierce their thin wrapper. The skull beneath the skin was as clear as a face at a window. His mouth remained open for so long that she feared the jaws might have sprung a bone.

Taggart dropped his heels, flicked open his eyes, and closed his mouth with an audible *snapp.* Sylvia could scarcely credit the transformation.

This new man was shorter than the original had been, even before the recent stretching. The joints had clicked back into their sockets, and the straying vertebrae had settled as snugly upon each other as a pile of counted coins. The deeply etched lines of stress across the brow and around the mouth had been smoothed away, but instead of making the face more amiable it gave the impression of belonging to a not-very-realistic dummy. The mouth hung slackly, as if the muscles which operated it had lost their texture. And the eyes! The eyes were windows in a derelict house.

Even the eyebrows seemed to indicate that she was about to deal with a different man. They now appeared to be about three centimetres higher up on his forehead, and she recalled another of Lavater's pronouncements about eyebrows. '*The more remote from the eyes, then the more volatile, easily moved, and less enterprising is the man.*'

'Well now!' said Sylvia with an assumed briskness, clapping her hands sharply together as if to impart some vitality to the lifeless figure. 'Let's go and find a saloon.'

She stood up, delighted to move her limbs again, and felt like skipping through the door. Taggart followed like a ghost.

CHAPTER SIXTEEN

When Will Forstell departed from Miss Bicknell he walked thoughtfully along the sidewalk in Thruway 1.

It went without saying that the experience had been a satisfying one. The selection, training and examination procedures of the aphrocollege meant that no graduate would ever give anything less than satisfaction. And yet, despite the memories which still warmed his loins, he felt irritably that the experience had, in some indefinable way, fallen short of his expectations.

That particular scenario had been a poor prelude. The memory of those moving clouds, the sliding river, the vivid greens and the shrill cries of birds, still afflicted him with nausea; and the aphrodolly herself, with her brown arms and strange scents, had seemed like a personal emanation of that unquiet scene. And lying deeper than this, almost too deep for acknowledgement, was his secret humiliation at having taken the soft option of going over to the First Sector by paveline and ringline, instead of braving the new hazards of taking an auto across the ring road and through the traffic circle.

Preoccupied by these thoughts, he looked up and saw a directional sign to the Autoterminus of the First Sector. When the building came into sight he directed his steps towards it.

The garden was similar to that outside the Autoterminus in the Second Sector. In this case some vagary of the civic planners had surrounded each tree with a decorative stahlex fence, although the items thus protected were neither removable nor damageable by any available human agency.

The Reception Area was also similar to the one he'd already seen. There were the same kinds of tables, chairs and credit counter. There was a similar series of antique two-dimensional pictures showing the evolution of the auto. The greatest difference was in the people.

As he might have expected if he'd thought about it, there were more aphrodollies here. This was their home ground, and their sector, after all. There must have been two or three dozen, on the lookout for potential clients who had just arrived by auto, and whom they might persuade to look no further. The Autoterminus in the Second Sector had contained only two or three, hoping to pick up clients on the way across. Will remembered his journey with Isabel and shuddered.

He wandered casually around the tables. He was given the flickering signal by a small Eskimo woman wrapped in skins, an Ibo girl with ritual scars carved into her black cheeks, and a Whig hostess who might have graced Holland House with her charm and wit.

There were more evident signs of wealth here, too, in the way people dressed and talked, and the self-confident way they comported themselves. The clothes were better cut, the vowels shorter and more clipped than they were in the Second Sector; and the self-assurance of the people here was so overpowering that Will felt as if he were being physically leaned upon.

He saw two piles of information booklets on a nearby table, picked up a sample of each rather furtively, and went out to find the paveline.

In the days to come, during those parts of his fractured life when he was free of work but hadn't accumulated sufficient credit to visit the First Sector, he now had something to do. He occupied himself by studying the two booklets.

He went on studying them for about two months.

The simpler of the two booklets was called *How To Drive An Auto*. There was an introduction, telling you that these electric autos didn't make any noise or fumes, and that on these and other grounds they were a welcome addition to the facilities of Tcity. This was followed by a general chapter, telling you how electric motors worked, and why the batteries had to be recharged from power points at each Autoterminus. Will wasn't interested in this kind of information, but was absorbed by the next chapter which got down to the kind of detail he wanted.

On the left-hand page was a picture showing the limited number of controls, instruments and indicators which appeared on the dashboard of the new autos, each one of which was identified by a circled number; and on the right-hand page the circled numbers were repeated sequentially with descriptions of what the items were for and how they should be used. A final page listed the various kinds of auto which were available, from the rectangular black box without doors (of which he already had experience), all the way up to the glittering silver shape which looked like a spaceship on wheels. He checked the hiring charges, and was able to confirm that it would cost all his increments for two months to hire one of the latter machines for a one-way trip between the two sectors.

He dedicated many evenings to the latter pages of this publication.

The other booklet was called *The New Autocomplex*, and upon cursory examination it struck him as much the more difficult of the two. After closer examination it struck him as so difficult as to be unintelligible.

The central double-spread pages contained a map of the new Autocomplex between the First and Second Sectors. There was an island which dozed like a bloated spider in the middle of a web too intricate for unravelling. Around the island was the traffic circle, and encircling the whole complex was a ring road. The traffic circle and the outer ring were connected by radial roads, so that any driver leaving the periphery was inevitably sucked in towards the centre. It frightened Will merely to look at the map.

As an aid to navigation the cartographer had drawn concentric circles round the island, and lettered them, so that there was some resemblance to a contour map. He couldn't understand it. The ring road was annotated also, with arrows and numbers. He couldn't understand that either. So whilst this two-page map helped to explain why he'd become so hopelessly lost on the trip with Isabel, it didn't make him feel that he would have any more success if he tried again.

The earlier pages of *The New Autocomplex* were devoted to explaining the letter codes of the contour lines round the central island. These letters were apparently intended to indicate the lanes which a driver should pursue in order to arrive at his destination in the terminus on the other side of the complex. The latter pages of the booklet contained illustrations of the different kinds of directional signs, warning signals and flashing lights, and explanations of what they meant. There was an appendix which contained a long series of numbered arrows, which presumably had something to do with the routes to be followed.

Will spent a large part of each evening staring at the central map and trying to memorize its more important features. He also pondered heavily upon the earlier and later sections of the booklet, in attempts to discover the meaning of the letter codes, the various signals and the arrows. The more frustrated he became the more angry he was, and the more angry he became the less he understood.

He told himself that he wasn't stupid; or at any rate, not all that stupid. He thought of those other young men, with the imitation stitches in the lapels of their jackets, their pink drinks in narrow-stemmed glasses, their superior short vowels and assumed American twang, who lounged so elegantly about the Reception Areas at each Autoterminus. If they could hire those silver and red autos and drive through the autocomplex as if it were the most natural thing in the world, then surely he could do the same in one of those wretched black boxes with open spaces where the doors ought to be.

Will spent evening after evening in a close scrutiny of

the two booklets. The time came round for his weekly visit to the First Sector, and still he didn't go. He persevered with his studies.

And still without success.

Almost two months had gone by without his paying his customary visit to the First Sector. The weeks passed without incident except that Greg Smythe, the Director of Depot Number Five, told him that he was to present himself shortly for an interview with some high-ranking female from outside the city. The appointment meant little to Will Forstell.

He whipped himself into a fever of application in his study of the booklets, particularly of the one which contained the central map, and finally gave up the struggle. With frenzied hands he tore up both booklets into tiny fragments, screwed the pieces together between his palms, and threw them into the incinerator.

OK! OK! OK! He was stupid! Stupid! Stupid! He stamped out of his module into the corridor, kicked the first passerby, and lost himself in the crowd.

While he travelled along the paveline in Thruway 5 he reminded himself of the unpleasant truth that all men were not equal. Some were cleverer than others. That meant they could obtain better jobs, earn higher increments, and do more exciting things than other men. They had better lives.

So what? As he circled the ringline he told himself that he earned sufficient increments to damn well enjoy himself once a week. And because of having stayed at home so long studying those unintelligible booklets, he had more than two months' increments to his credit.

By the time he reached Thruway 1 his ill temper had been dissipated by that unmistakable air of adventure and gaiety which always pervaded the First Sector. He looked at the huge dome of the Fun Palace, and reflected that his accumulated credit would enable him to go in just this once. The hurrying paveline bore him past while he was still thinking about it. When the triangular doorway of the Blue Star came up on the other side he actually took a step towards the slow lane. But he hesitated, and was swept onwards.

Will Forstell knew that his accumulated increments had given him sufficient credit to enter either of the big clubs. Common sense, however, reminded him that he wasn't really a big spender. He wasn't a director or a barber.

But at least he could buy himself a good time. He sidetracked into the slow lane and stepped on to the sidewalk.

CHAPTER SEVENTEEN

The speeding auto passed a sensor, and a huge electroluminous sign blazed above the autoway:

HATFIELD HOUSE – BARS & RESTAURANTS –
ALL USUAL ENVIRONMENT SUPPORTS –
ON LEFT IN 5 KMS.

Jan Caspol applied the brakes. Of a sudden nothing seemed more delightful than stretching his legs in fresh surroundings and having a drink. Besides, he thought, as he returned the auto to manual control, it would give him the opportunity of making good his ignorance of Buddhism before he met Arthur Medway.

He took the two-wheeled auto into the left-hand turn at high speed. The gyroscopes caused it to lean over at the correct angle, and eliminated any sensation of imbalance.

The autopark was crowded, but he guessed that all the other autos were dummies, placed there to make the Executive world appear less sparsely populated than it really was. The building looked very fine, with its warm Tudor bricks and big mullioned windows. Hatfield House had every sign of being a typical Executive autotel.

Jan entered a hall, the walls of which were hung with Spanish breastplates and Greenwich half-suits of jousting armour. The robo-manager came forward, walking as stiffly as if his shins were encased in a pair of ill-fitting greaves instead of immaculately tailored trousers.

'Good day, sir. Welcome to Hatfield House, where Elizabeth the First was sitting under an oak tree when she was first told that——'

'Don't tell me about it,' Jan said.

He followed a sign which said *Cecil's Bar* and found himself in a big Jacobean room with a minstrel's gallery and oriel window. The walls were decked with Brussels tapestries and paintings of bewigged Restoration Dukes by Lely or Kneller or someone of that kind. But these observations were incidental to the main enquiry, which was satisfied by the identification of a bar at the other end of the room, and he proceeded in that direction without delay.

The array of whisky studs was pleasantly varied, and after some happy deliberation he pressed for a Speyside malt. Life was rich and sweet.

'The cornice beneath the top of the bar,' a pre-recorded voice advised him, 'was almost certainly carved by Grinling Gibbons. You must bend down to see it properly, and you will then observe that——'

'Piss off!' Jan shouted. 'Piss off! Piss off!'

He sipped the golden end-product which had resulted from a mystic amalgam of soft water from the Scottish burns, Highland barley and the smoke of peat, matured for over ten years in old sherry casks. Life was good indeed. He perched on one of the high stools at the bar.

The room, like the autopark, appeared to be crowded. In this case the dummies were more sophisticated, and each of them could talk in a highly informed way about a limited number of topics. Selective use of them could give the lonely Executive the illusion that he was talking to members of his own class.

Jan knew that one of the autopals would soon be coming across to talk to him, so he thought he'd save time by ensuring it was the one he wanted. He found the button labelled *Hotel Control* and pressed it.

'Good day, sir. Welcome to Hatfield House where Elizabeth the First was sitting under a——'

'Don't start that again,' he said, managing to interrupt a little more quickly this time. 'I want somebody to talk to me about Buddhism.'

'Certainly, sir. Coming now, sir.'

Jan made himself comfortable on his stool. An autopal rose from its chair on the other side of the room, turned its head until its infra-red scanners registered the newcomer, and homed upon him without hesitation.

The figure was short and spare. Its head was modelled in conformity with the Bhikkhu stereotype: shaved cranium; shiny brown skin; bright eyes behind gold, round-rimmed spectacles; an enigmatic smile. It was wearing the yellow robe of Siam and Ceylon.

'I take refuge in Buddha,' it said.

'Why?'

The autopal was in full spate immediately. 'More than two billion people in the world today have moral standards which are derived from the teaching of a man who lived twenty-seven centuries ago. The Wheel of Samsara continues to turn, and——'

Jan interrupted. 'Cut out the general stuff. Let's get down to the Buddha's actual teaching.'

'Buddhas only point the way,' the autopal said. 'To begin with you should consider the Four Noble Truths. First there is the fact of sorrow, which arises from the realization that pleasure is fleeting whilst pain endures. Second is the discovery that the cause of sorrow is the desire for pleasure. Third is the acknowledgement that sorrow can be overcome by conquering selfish desires. Fourth is the knowledge of the Way of the Eightfold Path. You should also observe the Five Precepts. First, you must kill nothing. Second——'

'It's the Fifth Precept I find difficult,' commented Jan, finishing his whisky and pressing for another. 'But fill me in about the Eightfold Path.'

In less than a nanosecond the autopal had jumped its programme as instructed. 'The Way of the Eightfold Path tells us what is Right Doctrine, Right Motive, Right Speech, Right Conduct, Right Means of Livelihood, Right Effort, Right——'

'Forget about all the others,' he ordered, 'and tell me about the Right Means of Livelihood.'

Almost a microsecond, this time, as the autopal again skipped its programme. 'The Fifth Path, *Samma Ajiva*, tells us that we should select a trade or occupation which is compatible with the preceding four paths that I have just described at some length . . .'

Jan sniggered into his drink. Despite appearances, autopals couldn't help reminding you that they were machines.

'. . . always been a difficult thing to do. With the development of specialized skills, trade, money and technology, it became impossible. Think of a man doing a repetitive job on a lathe, which produced a component part for a machine assembled elsewhere; or the manager of a department in an organization so large that he was unaware of any general policy. Neither of these men had any means of knowing whether the results of their labours conformed with the Fifth Path. Although very few people in twentieth-century Europe and America were Buddhists, their inability to relate their individual means of livelihood to any ultimate good was the real cause of the malaise in business and industry. Then in the twenty-first century increasing mechanization and automation seemed about to solve all these problems. When it became unnecessary for a man to have any means of livelihood in order to live comfortably the Fifth Path was redundant. A person couldn't offend against the requirements of the preceding Four Paths by any activity in the Fifth, because the Fifth Path wasn't there any more.'

Jan nodded absently. The proposition sounded logical enough.

'But then something quite unexpected happened,' added the Bhikkhu. 'It became clear that some kind of economic activity is necessary, not for material but for spiritual reasons.'

'Okay,' Jan said. 'I know the rest of the argument.'

The autopal ignored him. 'The truths contained in the Way of the Eightfold Path are eternal ones. The Fifth Path continues to be essential to happiness and virtue. The god of another religion said "In the sweat of thy face shalt thou eat bread". We now see that this was not a curse on fallen man ejected from Eden, but a future condition of his spiritual health. When the Central Executive introduced the Work Project in the cities——'

'Stop! Stop!' Jan was waving his hands about in front of the gold-rimmed spectacles, and finally succeeded in transmitting some kind of message to the videcon scanners which they concealed. 'Give me a short run-down on Allington Castle and then I'll be going. But keep it *short*!'

A retrieval mechanism traversed, and located the appropriate index in the data bank.

'Allington Vihara is a centre of Theravada Buddhism. This is the oldest form of Buddhism, based on the Pali Canon, and its ascetic and intellectual philosophy has a great appeal to many Executives. Theravada has become increasingly distinguished from Mahayana Buddhism, which is more emotional, more reliant upon mere faith, and more inclined to promise some sort of heaven. It is not surprising that Mahayana has a greater appeal to the

Citizens. In its tantric forms it exploits the cult of Shiva and Kundalini, and encourages sensuality of a kind which——'

'Thank you,' Jan said, finishing his second whisky and banging the glass on the bar. 'That's enough.'

The Bhikkhu pressed its hands together, palm to palm, and bowed slightly as it backed away.

'Work out your own salvation with diligence. Remember that Buddhas only point the way.'

But Jan was already on his way.

CHAPTER EIGHTEEN

It wasn't until he actually sat down and started thinking about a map that Ozzie realized he didn't have any clear notion of how Aidan Beeblock was laid out. So far as other beeblocks were concerned, such as Oswald, which was the next one along, and Cuthbert, on the other side of the thruway, he'd never even set foot in them.

He decided that on his first leave-day he would devote the time to exploring the extent of floor 87 on which he lived.

Ozzie followed the one-way traffic along corridor 22, turned right into vestibule 712, and turned right again into corridor 21 so that he could proceed in the opposite direction and pursue an escalating number series. After a little while he had left behind the lower end of the 700 range, and was passing vestibules which he knew he had never entered. He was strongly tempted to enter them now, in the ever-present hope of coming across the annular archetype of his dreams, or at least of adding new specimens to his collection. With a deliberate effort of will he forced himself to pursue the specific objective he had set himself for today.

The number sequence of the vestibules continued – 801, 802, 803, 804 – with the odd numbers debouching into the corridor from the left, and the even numbers entering from the right. He began to wonder whether the vestibules would go on for ever, with the numbers growing so large that the ceiling indicators in the corridor wouldn't be able to contain all the digits.

On they went – 850, 851, 852, 853 – perhaps the numbers would grow so large that it would be impossible for anyone to remember his own address. A person living in the upper reaches of this corridor would need to have his vestibule number written down on an immensely long coil of paper, and he would have to keep unrolling and consulting it as he neared home. The vestibules continued – 891, 892, 893, 894 – but that would be absurdly clumsy. Perhaps it would be possible to memorize the first part of the number, and have only the second part written down. Say the number was 413790426. Then you would need to remember only . . . whatever the first three or four figures were, and have the rest written down.

It would be best to have the first three or four figures written down on another piece of paper, in case you forgot them. And it would be wise to carry duplicates in case you lost one.

On they went – 951, 952, 953, 954 – and the papers would have to be in different colours so that you could tell which part of the number they referred to. Say red for the first part and blue for the . . . No, that was no good. You would forget which colour was which. It would be best to have *First Part* printed on the back of the first part of the number and *Second Part* printed on the . . .

The vestibules continued – 990, 991, 992, 993 – but if the number was very long, and you'd memorized the first three or four figures and carried a reminder of that part which you consulted only if you forgot, then the second part of the number would be on a much longer piece of paper, probably in the form of a roll, and so it would be easy to . . .

What was it?

The question exploded as he came face to face with a blank wall. For a few blinding seconds his brain would do no more than register stupefaction.

After the initial shock he knew where he was. This was the end of the corridor, and he'd come up against the stahlex shell of Aidan Beeblock. He had entered a kind of corridor at right angles to corridor 21, and which he guessed joined the ends of all the other corridors in this beeblock. People coming up behind were shoving him and turning right or left into this end corridor. Thinking it odd that there should be a choice of direction, he turned to the right.

It was frightening to walk along that corridor and know that there was only a thin stahlex sheet between him and the outside air. He felt exposed and vulnerable, until he remembered that it wasn't really 'outside' air. On the other side of the stahlex sheet was the narrow space between Aidan and Oswald Beeblock, and it was filled with good, wholesome, filtered and processed air. The real 'outside' air was the air outside the city walls, full of dirt and germs. It was well known that a Citizen wouldn't live for long in that atmosphere.

What was happening?

This second question burst in his brain and wasn't as quickly answered as the first one. In front of him the corridor was crammed with people, which was a common enough sight, but what was extraordinary was that they were walking towards him. He'd never seen so many people from the front, never seen so many faces at one time. This opposition seemed to controvert a law so natural that he'd always taken it for granted. They came nearer, marching upon him in a murderous phalanx.

Terror froze the joints of Ozzie's limbs, and he stopped.

It would be more accurate to say that he would have stopped, had it not been for the people behind. They buffeted him and pushed him forwards. Just when it seemed that a head-on clash between the two parties was inevitable, Ozzie found himself borne to the right, where he mingled with the oncoming people who had swung to their left.

They were all walking together in the same direction, along a main corridor parallel to but in the opposite direction to corridor 21 along which he'd walked earlier in the day. Ozzie looked up at the ceiling indicators and noted the sequence of vestibule numbers – 998, 997, 996, 995 – and was daunted by the implications. He had a long walk ahead of him, and he was already tired and hungry. The numbers continued to decline – 951, 950, 949, 948 – and he realized that he must be back in corridor 22.

I am going towards zero, he thought, and a sudden onslaught of happiness turned his spine into a stick of ice and made him shiver with expectation.

The distant zero glittered in the grey wastes of his imagination. It started to swell, until its circumference was like the orbit of seagulls flying beneath a northern sky; it commenced to spin like a wheel, the circle of life and death which turns for ever; it began to shrink, until it was no larger than the jewelled ring of a Celtic cross. I am looking for a ring, he remembered.

I am a happy man, he decided.

He was also a very fatigued one, and so exhausted by the time he returned to his module that he scarcely had strength to press the button for *Today's Surprise.* He fell asleep with a piece of soyjoy on ryebread in his mouth.

The following day, after his return from the office, he wasted no time before applying his new knowledge.

He emptied one of the drawers in the sleeping-cubicle and labelled it *Fourth Sector.* He took a large folder, woven from stahlex fibre, and marked it *Aidan Beeblock.*

Then he took a smaller folder, with a flap, and inscribed it *Floor 87*.

Now he could prepare the first of the actual plans.

He did a good deal of measuring and arithmetic before he attempted to draw anything on paper. Even then he double-checked the simple calculations, and made numerous trial sketches, before he was prepared to begin.

His eyes were watering and his fingers were numb when he finally crawled into the bed. He drifted into that kind of delicious sleep which descends upon those who know that they have overtaxed their powers in a worthwhile cause. His dreams were made happy by images of that bright ring which was the object of his quest, and of which all the other items in his growing collection were mere anticipations.

He awoke very early, in accordance with his recently established custom, and had never felt so refreshed. He explored another vestibule on his way to the office. On the way back he had to fight a temptation to follow the shortest route, so anxious was he to recommence work on the plans.

As soon as he was in his module he took the papers and folders out of the drawer. With his tongue clenched between his teeth, his white forehead wrinkled with concentration, his fingers gripping a red crayon so tightly that his knuckles shone, he entered upon what was going to be one of the most satisfying parts of the entire quest.

Slowly, carefully, trembling with zeal to do the job as perfectly as was humanly possible, he began to colour those parts of the maps which indicated the corridors and vestibules which he'd already traversed.

He sorted the maps into sequence, placed them in the folder marked *Floor 87*, put that in the larger, open folder inscribed *Aidan Beeblock*, and dropped that into the drawer labelled *Fourth Sector*.

As he was about to close the drawer he had a new appreciation of the magnitude of the task he had undertaken, and of the miniscule extent of what he'd done up to now. There were all the other corridors (and he didn't know how many) on floor 87, each one presumably intersected by a thousand vestibules. There were all the other floors (and he didn't know how many) in Aidan Beeblock, each presumably with a similar number of corridors and vestibules.

Once he had covered all that ground he knew he must have found the ring which was the prime object of his quest; but he knew that a passion for completeness would then take possession of him, and drive him on to expand his collection. How many beeblocks were there in the Fourth Sector? Once again, he didn't know. The beeblocks followed each other along the sides of Thruway 4 as far as the eye could see.

Ozzie paused with his knees against the half-shut drawer, and closed his eyes the better to regard the inward, beatific vision which flooded his imagination.

His life stretched before him like an infinite panorama of fresh fields and verdant hills, an unending vista of lush valleys where morning mists added the enchantment of mystery to half-revealed delights.

The recurring excitement of following a different route to the office each morning, the almost intolerable suspense of turning into a fresh vestibule, would be duplicated every day as he made his way back to the module. And at home there would always be the devotional labour of crayoning his maps, and watching the branches of the vestibules sprout from the parental stems of the corridors, as red as the blood pumped out by his grateful heart.

From now onwards he put his campaign on an absolutely methodical basis. The maps, so painstakingly kept up-to-date, imposed an external discipline upon his hitherto somewhat random forays. Each morning he refreshed his memory by consulting the maps, and on his way to the office deliberately covered the next vestibules in sequence. This systematic method of working was rewarded almost immediately with a rhomboid handle from vestibule 512 off corridor 19, and coming home the same day he picked up a knob with concave finger-holds in vestibule 513 off the same corridor.

CHAPTER NINETEEN

Gloriana Schnurrbush hadn't been outside her module for years. It would have cost her too much effort, and would have been very hazardous besides.

When she moved she could feel her old bones grinding together like rusty nails in a bag. They were so brittle that an accidental kick on the shins would have made her legs shatter like glass. Her joints were so stiff that many times a day she expected them to seize up completely, so that she would be transfixed in some frozen posture like a figure in a picture – halfway out of bed, or half-risen from her chair, or just about to take a sip of tea.

'There is no reason for me to go out, is there?'

Dab sat at her feet, with his chin on her bony knees. Gloriana didn't simply mean that the autochef, the tri-di, the disposal chutes and the distribution system made it unnecessary to go out. She meant more than that. Dab looked up into her face with his big brown eyes. He seemed to understand.

'I have my memories,' she told him.

It wasn't until long after Steve had gone away, and she had reconciled herself to the unlikelihood of his ever coming back, that she realized what a miraculous gift memory was. Since that time she had spent most of her waking hours, and some of her sleeping ones, thinking about Steve. She relived the happy times they had spent together, and made the reality doubly certain by repeating the facts to Dab.

'It was going up and down that he liked,' she reminded him.

He wagged his tail two or three times and pulled his back legs into a more comfortable position. Once, when he was little more than a pup, Dab had escaped from the module and frisked out into vestibule 333. He had managed to drag himself back to the door with his hind legs trampled askew. The wounds had healed, but the left leg was permanently maimed, so that it dragged along behind his other hind leg. Gloriana loved him all the more because of his deformity.

'You'll never go out again, will you, Dab?' she asked, as she did several times a day.

He rubbed his chin on her knee and blinked his heavy Proustian eyelids to show that he agreed. He always did agree with her.

But Gloriana Schnurrbush always kept the outside door closed.

CHAPTER TWENTY

Sylvia led the way out into Thruway 1. When they were on the crowded sidewalk Taggart wavered about, this way and that. It seemed hardly possible that this irresolute creature could be the same man who'd been dealing so resolutely with people and affairs on the telephone such a little while before.

They were in danger of becoming separated. She seized him by the arm and halted outside the first saloon in the thruway.

'What about this?'

'I don't know,' he said. 'I always go to a bar in . . .'

Sylvia pushed him inside, steered him to a table, and went over to the bar to press for a couple of drinks and something to eat. As she thumbed the studs she observed that this was one of those strictly functional saloons, without environment supports, whose limited purposes caused her some unease.

There was nothing besides a plain stahlex bar with its rows of vending studs; a chequer-plate stahlex floor to provide adhesion for drunken feet; and spidery tables and chairs made out of featherlite tubes welded to the floor.

She returned to the table with two synthetic beers and a plate of angel biscuits. Taggart was wearing an expression of blank stupefaction.

'I've been here before,' he said, in a strange voice.

She looked at him quickly, more surprised by his agitation than by his remark. He became embarrassed.

'That's nice,' she said. 'Your health.'

Sylvia cautiously sipped the brown liquid, and grimaced despite her precaution. It was the unhealthiest stuff she'd ever tasted.

Taggart swallowed some beer and looked up at her; but he wasn't really looking at her. His eyes were as unfocused as those of a frog. In some strange, passive way, he seemed to have placed his trust in her.

'Don't you want to know what I'd like to talk to you about?'

He shrugged his shoulders, a movement so indefinite that it could have meant anything.

'All I know is that Mr Felixtowe told me you wanted to ask me some questions, and that I had to talk to you. I suppose I'll find out what it's all about without asking.'

Taggart waited dumbly, and gave every appearance of a man who would wait for ever rather than use any initiative. His shoulders were slumped, and his chest looked as if it had collapsed under the weight of the circumambient air.

Sylvia gazed at him in disbelief, almost with fear at this inexplicable change. She wouldn't have taken much convincing that Taggart had given her the slip in Thruway 1, and that she'd linked up with this other individual in error. Could this be the man whom she'd observed at work in his office not very long ago? That earlier man had been obsessed by the job in hand. Where was the firm, equable voice, the sharp eyes, the quiet self-confidence of the original?

The man who sat on the opposite side of this small table was an empty shell. He was as devoid of purpose as a lantern from which the light had been removed. And yet, she thought with some excitement, this might have some important bearing on the objectives of the Work Project.

'It was kind of you,' she started again, 'to come and have a chat with me.'

'I do what I'm told,' the dead voice informed her.

'What I wanted to ask you was a few questions about your motives for working.'

Taggart stared sightlessly at the opposing walls. 'My motives?'

'Ye-es.' Her laugh broke the word in two, attempting to establish the conversation in a lighter mode. 'Let me come straight out with it. Why do you work?'

He lowered his eyes to the table top, and slowly brought them into focus on a small pool of spilled beer. He dipped his finger in the brown liquid and started drawing circles with it. Round and round went his finger, first clockwise, and then anti-clockwise, as if to avoid upsetting some mystical balance of forces. Round and round and back again.

'For example,' she prompted, 'you might work for money?'

His finger continued to go round and round on the

top of the table. Like the seagulls at Lindisfarne, she thought.

'I know the state annuity makes it unnecessary for anyone to work,' she said, agreeing with the obvious point that he hadn't bothered to make. 'Anyone can live in . . . comfort, without doing a stroke of work, and that's the way many people like to be.'

Taggart began a new series of concentric circles, each one larger than the one before. He might have been deaf.

'But some people feel they would like a little bit extra. They think it's worth working for the increments so that once in a while they can live like a barber.'

She used the city colloquialism rather self-consciously. It was a slightly wry joke in the Executive world that their continuing failure to automate some very old trades, such as the barbering of hair and the picking of grapes, had transformed what were once humble practitioners into a rich élite among the Citizens . . . In France they said *vivre comme un vendangeur.*

'Some pleasures are still expensive,' she said, and recalled, not without displeasure, the stories Jan had told her about the flicker circuit in the First Sector. 'Some men, for example, like to be able to go into the big clubs now and again.'

Taggart stopped his doodling on the table top. 'I'm not interested in aphrodollies. I think they're unnatural.'

'Of course!' She was delighted to have drawn a response from him. She was also secretly delighted with his sentiments although she was fully familiar with the college's argument: their graduates were merely trained to exercise natural functions at their highest physiological potential. 'Of course!' she repeated. 'But people want money for other reasons. They might want a bit extra to——'

He interrupted. 'I'm not interested in money. I don't want anything I haven't got.'

'You're a lucky man.'

Sylvia lifted her tankard and tilted her head in a pretence of drinking the synthetic poison which served as beer in the cities. Over the stahlex rim she observed the lines of stress return to Taggart's brow, and then wash away again to leave the dead, waxen mask. The eyebrows, high on the forehead, maintained their defiance of Lavater's thirty-fifth physiognomical rule.

'What about power?'

'What about it?'

'Perhaps you work because you have a desire for power.'

'I don't see what power has to do with it.'

She tried to show the connection. 'If people work they have authority relationships with other people. If they work hard they increase their chances of promotion. If they are promoted they have more authority over other people. It's the enjoyment of power that makes them work, and the desire for more power that makes them work harder.'

As she talked, Sylvia relived the pleasure she had derived from studying the old industrial psychologists with the Executives of the Stahlex Corporation. As Chief Executive of Tcity, she was a member of the Central Executive, and had been an enthusiastic proponent of the Work Project to which the Stahlex Corporation had given its support.

The evolution of the various schools of industrial psychology had fascinated her.

The views of Malthus had dominated the nineteenth century. People were animals who worked in order to provide themselves with the necessities of life: food, clothing, shelter. If they didn't work hard enough to please their masters they were thrown into the streets to die of starvation or exposure. The spectre of an arithmetic increase in food supplies accompanied by a geometric increase in population haunted economic theory.

'The desire for power isn't necessarily bad,' she continued. 'You have a position of some authority, haven't you?'

Taggart barely nodded his head.

In the twentieth century there had been a revulsion against this carrot-and-stick philosophy. As the century progressed the state helped to provide its citizens with the three necessities of life for which nineteenth-century man had been obliged to work so hard. Increasing affluence meant that people could satisfy their basic requirements with relative ease.

In that century Maslow had shown that man's needs could be depicted in a kind of hierarchy, which could in turn be represented by a triangle. At the base were the purely animal needs of self-preservation – sleep, hunger, thirst, shelter and so on. When one need was satisfied the next one emerged, and when they were all satisfied they ceased to be important. When man had satisfied his lower-order needs, then higher-order needs presented themselves for fulfilment. Herzberg showed that poor working conditions, bad personal relationships and low pay made people dissatisfied; but he also argued that superior working conditions, good personal relationships and high pay, whilst removing the dissatisfactions, did not of themselves make people want to work. Men wanted satisfaction from the actual job. The intrinsic as well as the extrinsic factors had to be right.

Both Maslow and Herzberg, in their different ways, were saying the same thing. Man is indeed an animal, but an animal of a special kind. He is an animal with spiritual aspirations.

'Your advice and decisions have some influence on the success or failure of Depot Number One. You have a number of subordinates whom you tell what to do. Many people in your position would have a feeling of power, and would enjoy exercising it, even if unconsciously.'

'I don't know what you're talking about,' he said. 'I just do my job and try to get along with people. That's all there is to it.'

Sylvia smiled, trying not to show her exultation. She

pretended to finish her own beer, collected Taggart's empty tankard, and returned to the bar. As she pressed the stud for a single refill, she reflected that she had probably found her first man who justified the Work Project. None of the old primary lusts seemed to motivate him; nor, she guessed, did any of their sub-categories, such as money for its own sake or power as a game. She returned to the table with a new confidence which exhilarated her. Soon she would have her first solid evidence that the Work Project was a success in Tcity.

Taggart reached for the replenished tankard without looking up.

'Have you heard of Yutaka Kimura?' she asked.

He shook his head and drank.

'He was a psychologist of the twenty-first century.'

'Why tell me?'

Sylvia pretended to sip the revolting liquid, and thought about her next move.

Yutaka Kimura had been an Industrial Relations Consultant to the monolithic Japanese steel industry in the previous century. He had one of the most perceptive minds of his time, and had clearly foreseen the impending social crisis. It was he who had first clearly stated the need for a new industrial psychology.

Kimura had reminded people that the changed conditions of the twentieth century, with increased state welfare services and higher standards of living, had satisfied those basic needs which had once made people work. Malthus and the industrial psychology of the nineteenth century had been made irrelevant.

He also showed that the changed conditions of the twenty-first century, with its increasing mechanization and automation, would soon satisfy the secondary desires of mankind: in particular the provision of leisure and a wider choice of leisure activities. Up to this point he was, more or less, documenting the theoretical work of Maslow and Herzberg.

Sylvia noticed that Taggart was steadily eating his way through the plateful of angel biscuits. She tried one herself, and choked on what felt like a mouthful of sawdust. Jan sometimes repeated a joke of one his old friends, who'd said that angel biscuits would destroy any ambition a man might have to go to Heaven.

But Kimura then went on to argue that two trends would soon be identifiable. On the one hand people with little capacity for general education and without required skills would soon have ample leisure, although they were the very people least fitted to occupy their leisure in ways which Kimura thought desirable. On the other hand the better-educated minority, who could have used their leisure to good effect, would be deprived of such activities because they would be part of a managerial class, and be forced to work longer and longer hours in an attempt to direct increasingly complex operations.

Yutaka Kimura wasn't listened to, either in his own country or in the West. When the solution did come, in the twenty-second century, it was by means which he hadn't foreseen and of which he mightn't have approved. Genetic medicine and brain surgery had created the Executive class, which had solved the problems in its own way.

Sylvia had managed to choke down half an angel biscuit. 'Yutaka Kimura was a very interesting man,' she began, 'and it's a pity he wasn't a more influential one. His new theory of why people should work was a metaphysical and not a pragmatic one.'

'I don't understand words like that.'

She forced a smile. Talking to Citizens was such a tedious business.

'His theory would take a long time to explain. But his message was that "a man needs to work in order to become truly himself." By this he meant that if a man——'

She was interrupted by a metallic clang. Taggart had

leaped to his feet and banged his tankard on the table. Some of the beer slurped out.

'He was a fool!' he shouted. 'Whatever he meant, he was a fool!'

Sylvia looked up at him in astonishment. The dead body of the man had been reanimated by some demoniac power. Forgotten muscles jumped to life as if they were being galvanized. His face was distorted by rage and pain, with the eyes round and staring, and the mouth working convulsively under the stress of some incommunicable passion.

'He was a fool!' he shouted again. 'A fool! A fool! A fool!'

He emphasized the phrase by crashing his tankard on the table with every repetition, and the remains of the beer were thrown over his shoulder and down his back. Then he stood silently, clenching the handle of the lowered tankard and shaking violently. She could hear the bottom of the tankard rattling against the table.

'Sit down,' she whispered. 'Please.'

He sat down as suddenly as if his hamstrings had been severed. The blood crept away from his face, and the white skin would have been that of a dead man if it hadn't glittered with sweat. Drinkers at the other tables, whose attention had been attracted by the scene, now lost interest and turned away.

'I'm sorry,' she said, quietly. 'I obviously said something that distressed you, although I can't imagine what it was. I'm sorry.'

The man's eyes were lifeless once again, and his mouth hung as loosely as before. Only his hands, which lay on the table with their twisting fingers interlinked, retained some vital tension.

'You still want to know why I work?' asked the dead voice.

Sylvia nodded. She felt that she now had very little control over the dialogue.

'I'll tell you. What was it the Japanese psychologist said, whoever he was?'

'Yutaka Kimura,' she reminded him, and quoted the dictum again. ' "A man needs to work in order to become truly himself." '

'That's it. Well I work for precisely the opposite reason.'

She was quite lost now, and must have shown it by her expression.

'I need to work in order to become anybody or anything that isn't truly myself. I would do anything, *anything*, not to be myself. I used to try drink and drugs until the Work Project came along. Work is better than any of them.'

She waited, wondering, horrified.

'I work to escape from myself.' Taggart put his hands on the sides of his head. 'For a few frantic hours a day, while I'm at work, I lose myself completely. In fact it's even better than that. I worry about my work even after I get home, and that helps as well.'

'I see,' she said.

'No you don't! You can't possibly see because you don't understand.'

Sylvia flushed. She had been trying to limit herself to words of one syllable, and had conscientiously avoided the metaphors, the tropes, the endless cultural analogies and references which were the spontaneous parlance of the Executives, and which had developed into a species of twenty-second-century euphuism. It was an unusual situation for her. Particularly as Taggart was right: she didn't understand.

'I don't understand it myself,' he said, and beat the side of his skull with his fist. 'The more I am forced to use whatever is inside here the more I escape from it.'

She responded tentatively. 'A desire to escape from the self is nothing new. It goes back at least as far as Buddha.'

'Buddha?'

'You have many Mahayana temples in Tcity. One of the doctrines is that by contemplation a man can escape——'

The lifeless voice interrupted. 'None of those religions are any use to me. They are only another kind of drug. I must have something stronger.'

'Your work?'

'When I go to work in the morning and hear the telephone ringing for me before I even open the door, then I am thankful. It is like a call from another world. It makes me forget about the things that have happened in this one.'

'What things?'

Taggart's face stiffened, and he clenched his hands tightly together on the table. She saw his fingers turn white as he twisted them against each other.

'What things? What things are you trying to forget?'

He was on his feet again, so quickly that he almost overbalanced and gripped the table for support. 'Shut up! Keep quiet! It's difficult enough when I'm away from work, without you asking your filthy questions!'

'But I'm only——'

'Shut up! Shut up!'

'But I only want to——'

With a loud yell Taggart clapped his hands over his ears and ran out of the saloon.

Sylvia sat still for a while, staring at her synthetic beer and the half-eaten angel biscuit. Could it really be a world of only chemicals and sawdust? She looked at her chrono, stood up and brushed the crumbs from her skirt.

She had an appointment in the Fifth Sector with someone called Will Forstell.

CHAPTER TWENTY-ONE

City walls appeared on the horizon, and grew rapidly in height as the auto sped towards them.

The autoway swept eastwards in a broad arc. Jan looked out at the dark shadows of a city which had entered history after the Claudian invasion and which, after a period of world importance, history had now left behind. It was like another Carthage which time had spared. Somewhere near the centre was the square mile of the original city, which had been bounded by the stone walls of the Romans; now the whole sprawling city was hidden behind the stahlex walls erected by a far mightier race.

From the evidence available it had always seemed to Jan Caspol that London, despite its previous fame, had never possessed more than a second-hand claim to greatness. It had for a time been the most powerful city in the world for reasons which had nothing to do with its own virtues: it happened to be the capital city of a country where provincial towns and areas had at different times been world leaders in breeding cattle, mining coal, making cloth, developing railways, manufacturing iron and steel; it had, inevitably, become the capital and *entrepôt* of the largest and richest empire which had ever existed.

London itself had produced little apart from paper and biscuits.

Illustrated catalogues of London's departed glories showed that even its architecture was second-hand at best, and often derived at third- or fourth-hand through the distorting mirror of continental Europe. Politics was Gothic, as in the Houses of Parliament; but learning was Greek, as in the British Museum. Within these broad extremes fancy was allowed to run riot.

Jan curled up comfortably in the driving seat, thought about the historical catalogues, and exercised his faculties of total recall.

The Temple of Diana at Ephesus was the ancestor of Decimus Burton's Athenaeum, and the Temple of Vesta at Tivoli had fathered a corner of Soane's Bank of England; John Nash took the Marble Arch from the Arch of Constantine in Rome, and Nelson's Column was copied from one of the Corinthian columns in the Temple of Mars; Inigo Jones designed the Banqueting Hall in Whitehall with Palladio's book of rules in his hand, and Gilbert Scott's government offices on the other side were stolen from the Italian Renaissance; the patent stucco of Robert Adam's façades was taken from Pompeii, and the polychrome interiors of Butterfield's churches were borrowed from Venice; the baroque of Vienna and Prague furnished the Central Hall in Westminster and...

What a stupefying experience it must have been to wander around those disorderly streets. People must have felt as if their brains were being scrambled in an architectural kaleidoscope which was given a thorough shaking every time they turned a corner.

The walls of London dwindled away on the right and disappeared behind him.

All those crazy things had gone now, except for Wren's Byzantine dome which sat on top of a beeblock in one of the eastern sectors. It was a reminder of an age when talents were allowed to express themselves with the freedom of weeds, not subject to any control or direction. But they did create things, Jan thought uneasily.

The auto fled into the round black mouth of a tunnel under the Thames, and the headlights came on automatically to confirm its empty length.

He lay back in the self-profiling seat and luxuriated in the sensation of being part of a perfectly engineered machine. Even after 200,000 kilometres and no maintenance the gas turbines ran without vibration and in total silence. He opened a side screen. Even in the tunnel the only noise was from the stahlex-wire reinforced tyres, with the faint suggestion of a whisper from the vents which scooped up the air for mixing with the waste heat brought forward by the heat exchangers.

His imagination repeopled this deserted tunnel with the travellers of a previous age. He tried to picture the queues of stationary cars en route to the coastal resorts or the Continent, their piston engines vomiting carbon monoxide, carbon dioxide and the oxides of nitrogen from thousands of noisy exhausts, while their primitive air-conditioners laboured in vain to clean the atmosphere inside each vehicle. It constricted his breathing merely to think of it, and he was glad to leave the tunnel and its ghosts behind.

The autoway approached a slender bridge suspended on stahlex wires which glistened like spiders' webs in the declining sun, and crossed the sparkling waters of the next river. Another walled city sprawled around the estuary, and then the autoway skirted a chalk scarp of the North Downs.

A green light on the control panel had started to wink at measured intervals, indicating that the auto would stop in ten kilometres unless new co-ordinates were punched in.

Jan looked down through the panoramic screen. Below him were the hop-fields, with their trellises of bines and circular oast-houses, which flavoured natural beer of the Executives. Beyond them were the ancient orchards, which graced Executive fruit-bowls with fresh cherries, strawberries, peaches, apples and pears.

The light started to wink amber. Only five kilometres to go. The autoway dipped away from the chalk escarpment, and the auto followed it downwards. He touched the brakes lightly, and looked ahead.

The plain of the Weald rolled away to the distant horizon, above which the early evening sky was streaked with hectic red and rich orange which could have come from the brush of Alençon. Romney sheep lazed in the luscious meadowland.

The light winked red. He immediately took over manual

control and applied the brakes hard. Within a few metres a sign *Allington Castle* pointed him off the autoway, and he turned sharp right. The two-wheeled auto leaned acutely into the bend, with the gyroscopes maintaining perfect balance and steering.

Crenellated towers appeared above some tall elms, and after another turn in the narrow road he brought the auto to a halt on a gravelled drive. The auto door was still closing behind him when an elderly but erect figure approached from the shadows of the gatehouse.

'I take refuge in Buddha.'

Jan scrunched forward with his hand extended.

'Arthur. How promptly you welcome your guests.'

The other man gave a slight smile. 'All done by an infra-red scanner which is directed through a peephole in the main gate, and which activates a warning bell. A typical monkish device.'

Arthur Medway, the salutation over, slowly retraced his steps. Jan followed, observing the erect figure, and the clear white flesh of one shoulder which appeared above the saffron robe. He was still conscious of the welcoming handshake and the smile. The handshake had been firm, with a brief extra pressure which conveyed something of its own certain strength. The smile was somehow firm too, as if confirming the steadfast assurance which appeared in the level gaze.

They went through the door of the gatehouse, and then through a smaller door on the right.

'This was the Porter's Lodge,' Arthur said, 'but it was incorporated in the chapel a long time ago.'

He pointed at a statue of a black madonna carved out of bog oak, drew attention to a niche decorated with Persian tiles, and commented on various pieces of bric-à-brac which had belonged to the castle's many previous owners. Jan nodded, asked a few questions, and followed his host into the main body of the chapel.

'You see that our chapel is quite bare.'

Their feet slapped against the stone floor, and echoed with a hollow noise in the empty nave. The flat, naked walls were washed white, and were interrupted only by the plain glass of the windows.

'If this were one of the Mahayana temples in the cities,' said Arthur Medway, 'the walls would be covered with murals. They would show incidents in the Buddha's previous lives from the Jataka stories; legends of his birth, youth, marriage and enlightenment from the poems of Ashvaghosha; and moral fables from the popular Sutras. If it were a Neochristian Adventist church there would be pictures of the faithful making the way straight for the Second Coming of Christ in his starship, in accordance with the instructions of Isaiah. In the same way the medieval cathedrals used sculptures or similar means to show the fourteen stations of the cross, and coloured windows to illustrate the lives of the Holy Family and the saints.'

Arthur continued his slow deliberate walk. 'The simple-minded,' he added, 'have always needed plenty of incident if their attention was to be held for more than five minutes. This is the case with their religion, just as with their other fictions.'

Jan looked at him quickly, and looked away again. The words would have sounded harsh, had it not been for the gentle voice and the smile. He knew that he would always remember the smile when he thought about Arthur Medway.

'We are all Desdemonas at heart,' Jan said. 'We all like to hear of "most disastrous chances, of moving accidents by flood and field, of hairbreadth scapes i' the imminent deadly breach".'

They had reached the end of the chancel, where a small Buddha *Rupa* was sitting in the earth-touching gesture.

'I'm afraid you're right, Jan. Even we are incapable of delivering "a round, unvarnished tale." He gestured towards the base of the figure, where some freshly cut flowers had been strewn before it. 'Even we need some small aids to thought and contemplation.'

Arthur Medway opened a door. They passed through, and descended a flight of steps into a courtyard. The ancient ragstone walls were almost hidden by climbing roses. As Jan's feet traversed the smooth lawn he had the sensation of having entered another world. Here was a more profound experience of peace than he had ever encountered.

They were approaching a Tudor door. Above the arch Jan saw the small statue of a figure on a horse.

'Who's that up there?'

'Above the arch? That's St Martin of Tours.'

'You don't seem to mind having the totems of other religions around the place.'

The monk's face showed his peaceful inward smile. 'The Buddha didn't object to Hinduism twenty-seven centuries ago. So I'm sure we can tolerate a Christian saint who divided his cloak and gave half to a beggar.'

'Like our own St Aidan. He gave King Oswald's horse to a beggar.' Jan reinforced the point facetiously, by poking at Arthur's bare shoulder. 'Not half a horse. A *whole* horse.'

Arthur Medway laughed quietly, and they entered the inner courtyard. The refurbished plaster and lath of a Tudor house made Jan suddenly aware of the grey slate of the courtyard they had just left.

The monk produced something from his pocket and threw it on the ground. A flock of pigeons descended with clapping wings, and shouldered each other as they fed.

'What extraordinary birds!' Jan said. 'I've never seen pigeons that were brown all over.'

'Nor will you see them anywhere else. They are descended from the original stock which Sir Thomas Wyatt brought here from Italy.'

Jan extended his arms, and addressed the feeding pigeons:

'Sighs are my food; my drink they are my tears;
Clinking of fetters such music would crave:
Stink and close air away my life wears;
Innocency is all the hope I have.'

Arthur nodded appreciatively. 'He wrote that in the Tower of London. However I much prefer the lines he wrote to John Poins, in which he explained how he hated the hypocrisy of life in London, and much preferred to be here at Allington:

This maketh me at home to hunt and hawk;
And in foul weather at my book to sit;
In frost and snow, then with my bow to stalk:
No man doth mark whereso I ride or go:
In lusty leas at liberty I walk.'

'It certainly scans better than my sample,' Jan said.

'Whatever his shortcomings as a poet, let us not forget that he brought the Italian sonnet to England, just as he introduced these birds.' Arthur threw some more Indian corn on the ground, and the birds shuffled against each other with increased animation. 'I never look at these brown pigeons without thinking that the effects of the Italian Renaissance are still too much with us.'

'In what way?'

The monk was about to respond, but then smiled and changed his mind.

'Let us talk about that later. I have been discourteous in keeping you from your dinner for so long.'

Arthur Medway led the way back with slow deliberate strides. He took a short step and then a long one, in order to avoid a hairy red caterpillar which was in their path. Jan did likewise. It was the First Precept.

CHAPTER TWENTY-TWO

Will Forstell went into the very first saloon he came across in the First Sector. The insignia of the aphrocollege winked at him from all sides. He bought himself a synthetic beer and a kickstick, and walked up and down puffing yellow smoke, so as to be able to look round at his leisure.

After some internal debate, second thoughts and backward turning, he finally came to a halt in front of a girl wearing a purple sari.

'What's your name?'

'Vajra-Yogini.'

Perfect white teeth shone at him from the dark face. Black, slightly oblique eyes appraised him from above high Mongolian cheekbones.

'What's your scene, Vagini?'

'I am coming from a very nice Tibetan temple.'

It didn't sound very exciting. 'What d'you do there, Vagini?'

'I am studying Tantras.' She moved a little closer to him. 'All the time I am studying Tantras.'

Vajra-Yogini was very small, and now that she was so close she had to look up at him.

'What are they?'

'They are Buddhist scriptures which are describing in great detail rituals which must be practised most assiduously in order to achieve true enlightenment.'

Will was held by a gleam in her dark eyes. 'Rituals such as what?'

'There are mudras, which are gestures with fingers and hands. There are mantras, which are verbal incantations. And there are yantras, which are symbolic diagrams. All these rituals are having magic power. All are important, because they set the mind free from its prison.'

It sounded even more dull than he'd thought. He didn't want to waste the evening.

'I haven't come over here to do any studying,' he said, thinking of *How To Drive An Auto* and *The New Autocomplex*. 'I've done enough of that over the last few weeks.'

The teeth shone again, and the gleam in her eye was less ambiguous. 'You are not having to study anything. I am learning enough tantric ritual for us both. I am knowing the mudras –' she made a half-closed fist – 'the mantras' – she made a circle with her mouth – 'and the yantras' – she made a gesture which was part of the *lingua franca* of all races. 'I am sharing my magic with you.'

Vajra-Yogini took his hand. Her fingers were so slender, and the bones in them so fine, that he was sure he could have snapped them off with a sudden movement.

'Come with me,' she said. 'We shall be reaching enlightenment together. Not only once but many, many times.'

She led him to the back of the saloon, through a doorway and along a short passage which issued into a main corridor. After only a few steps she opened a module door, found his hand and pulled him inside.

'Not far,' said Will, who had on occasion been obliged to walk very long distances.

Her teeth gleamed. 'The path to true enlightenment is short for those who know the right way.'

The cubicle was completely without furniture or decoration. He was vaguely disappointed, not having known what to expect anyway, and he looked around for finger-holds in the walls to see where chairs could be unfolded.

'Please be sitting down.'

He was still studying the walls. 'Where?'

'On the floor please.'

He sat down awkwardly, feeling foolish and at a disadvantage.

She pushed his legs and flexed his knees into a different posture, and rearranged his hands on his lap. It wasn't a position he would have chosen, but he was surprised to find that it wasn't uncomfortable. He was about to ask what happened next when the light went out.

The silence was interrupted by a recorded voice.

'Think of Shiva, the God of Destruction and the Lord of Regeneration, until you feel his image swelling inside you.'

He noticed that a faint illumination was beginning to brighten the walls, and he thought he could see indistinct shapes on their surfaces. He became aware of a musical rhythm beneath the recorded voice, so faint that it might have been nothing more than a vibration on the floor. Of Vajra-Yogini there was no sign. He could understand that her purple sari would have made her almost invisible in the total darkness, but the increasing illumination of the walls would soon reveal her.

'Let your body become a palace, in which all the windows are ablaze with the glory of the God Shiva who dances inside.'

The walls were brighter, and he could see that the shapes were those of human beings, or perhaps of gods who resembled human beings. The musical rhythm had acquired a more insistent beat. A faint scent touched his nostrils, and he looked round for the girl.

'You have the outward shape of Shiva, but now you are as big as a module. You grow larger, and now you are the size of a beeblock.'

Vajra-Yogini appeared before him. She had thrown aside the purple sari. The dark tones of her flesh were relieved by silver bracelets round her wrists and ankles.

'Now you are shrinking again. You return to your normal

size. Then you grow smaller, and smaller still, until you are the size of a crumb from an angel biscuit.'

She began to move, slowly, in time with the insistent rhythm of the music. Bells on her anklets and bangles started to tinkle. Now that the rhythm was more distinct, he noticed that the illumination waxed and waned in phase with the loudness and softness of the music. A more heady wave of perfume reached his nostrils. He saw that the figures on the walls were male and female, dancing together.

'The Goddess Kundalini, who has been curled inside your perineum, awakens like a serpent. She unfolds, stretches herself and yawns. An unexpected rapture burns with a hot flame four fingers below your navel.'

The music became louder and quicker. Vajra-Yogini was dancing more energetically, but to some different rhythm which didn't coincide with that of the music. The bells on her wrists and ankles tinkled more insistently. The lights in the walls also went out of phase with the music, sometimes shining with painful brightness, and switching on and off at random intervals. The aroma of the scent was very powerful, and with every inhalation he could feel it against the back of his throat.

'After ten more breathings the fire will have moved downwards, even to the ends of your toes.'

The beat of the music made his legs tremble, and the flashing of the lights made him blink. Sometimes the girl's face appeared before him like a lamp suspended in the darkness, with a beam of bright light eliminating all her features except the black eyes: at such times even the shadows below her Mongolian cheekbones disappeared, and her face was as flat as the features on an old penny.

Sometimes the beam of light would be lowered and he could see nothing but her legs below the knee, tapering towards the silver chains and finely boned feet, dancing out of time to the music. Sometimes the writhing torso appeared, headless and limbless, glistening with sweat as if coated in honey.

'After ten more breathings the fire will have moved upwards, to the crown of your head and even to the tips of your fingers.'

The deep musical chords continued to sound, reverberating in the floor, resonating in his bones, sometimes seeming to exist only inside the bony shell of his own head. All semblance of harmony had disappeared. From time to time the chord was fractured, and its musical components were dispersed in a thousand directions. When that happened the light was splintered into hundreds of sparkling shards, which rippled like escaping water over the girl's shining body and the walls of the cubicle. The figures on the walls came to life under that dappled light, and Will saw the god and the goddess coupling together in ecstasy.

The fleeing musical elements were recaptured and organized into a series of unbalanced chords. The scattered particles of light were reassembled into a narrow beam, which moved every time a chord was struck. The beam of light traversed the girl's figure erratically, illuminating first one part and then another: neck, thighs, pelvis and stamping feet, so that they appeared to be not parts of the same woman, but the dismembered pieces of many.

'Now you have the strength of Vishnu the Preserver. The strength of ten incense-exhaling divine elephants is only one hundredth of the strength of Vishnu the Preserver. But you are he!'

He tried to stand up, but wondered whether his legs would be too numb to support him. He found that he already was standing up, and probably had been for some time. He also discovered that his legs were moving in a hopeless attempt to keep time with the irreconcilable rhythms of the music, the light, and the girl's dancing feet.

So the Goddess Kundalini ascended to her Lord in the pericarp of the Thousand-Petalled Lotus. Around the four walls of the cubicle the God Shiva ravished his consort in a tantric ritual of unending bliss.

And Will Forstell staggered forwards to the only form of enlightenment he could ever know.

CHAPTER TWENTY-THREE

That evening, his eyes red with fatigue and his fingers numb from holding the crayon, Ozzie put his maps in the drawer labelled to receive them. As always these days, he paused with the drawer half-closed, and shut his eyes the better to regard that internal landscape which gave a pattern to his entire existence.

It wasn't there!

The thought struck him between the eyes like a bony fist. He would never do it!

All those vestibules and all those corridors, all those floors and all those beeblocks! His imagination swelled as it tried to accommodate the gigantic picture. It failed. He realized, for the first time, that at his present rate of progress he would be an old man before he moved on from Aidan Beeblock. He would have found the ring, he supposed, which had revolutionized his life and which was almost certainly on this floor. But he would be dead long, long before he finished his appointed journey.

Ozzie bowed his head in despair and opened his eyes. He looked into the half-closed drawer at the folder which contained the maps of his explorations. There was only one decision he could make, if this life had any meaning. He made it.

He was frightened by what he had to do. That night he lived through dozens of versions of the approaching scene. He awoke almost too exhausted to slide out of bed.

At the office he procrastinated until he feared that some business requirement might cause Mr Amory to leave early. This would subject him to another night of torment and another wasted day. The dread of this double misery drove his unwilling legs up the steep stairway and, more slowly, along the passage at the top.

Ozzie tapped on the smooth stahlex surface of the door, and heard a growling voice on the other side which might have been telling him to come in.

He tapped again to make sure.

'Come in! Come in!'

Ozzie cringed.

'Come in! Come in for Christ's sake!'

He eased the door open, just wide enough for his ingress if he turned sideways. He squeezed inside like a sliver of warmed butter.

'What d'you want?' demanded Mr Amory.

Ozzie blinked, looked around the room, and gaped. He'd never seen such a large area of unoccupied space in his life. It was the only office without wall mirrors he'd ever seen, but even so the impression of space made him feel giddy. Mr Amory's desk alone, which looked as if it were made of wood, was wider than the Filing Department.

'Good morning... Good afternoon, sir. I wanted to...'

'Well?'

This was another world. Mr Amory, sitting behind the big desk, with his large head and broad shoulders, was something more than a mere man. Tentrix was standing beside him, with her notebook open. Her depraved eyes were like ash-filled craters on some volcanic planet.

'What d'you want?' shouted Mr Amory.

'Well, sir. I sort of . . . sort of wanted to leave.'

'What d'you mean? Leave what?'

Ozzie was sweating, but immensely relieved that he was almost there. 'Leave here, sir.'

'Go on then,' said Mr Amory. 'Bugger off. Nobody asked you to come here in the first place.'

'Thank you, sir.'

Ozzie bowed his compliance and backed towards the door. The episode had been shorter, and much more painless, than in any of his previsions of it.

But now Tentrix was bending over to say something into Mr Amory's ear, and pointing at some item in the big diary on his desk.

'Wait a minute!' commanded Mr Amory. 'Are you employed here?'

Ozzie's voice almost lost itself, choked off by the expression on Mr Amory's face.

'Yes, sir. At least I was until you so kindly told me to——'

'What's your name?'

'Ozzie, sir. That is to say, Osbert Osborne, sir.'

Mr Amory scrutinized the entry in his desk diary, and turned towards Tentrix. 'Is this right?'

Tentrix, who had been staring at Ozzie with bold, enquiring eyes, nodded her head. 'Yes. He works in the Filing Department.'

Mr Amory stood up, supporting himself on the desk with the huge, spreadeagled fingers of his massive hands. He was almost twice as tall as Tentrix.

'What do you want to leave for?'

The question was direct, but not as demanding as it

might have been, and it was intermixed with some element of genuine concern. An expression of curiosity flickered in the eyes of the girl.

'I just feel that I'd rather sort of leave.'

'But why?' asked Amory, showing signs of exasperation. 'Work is the new therapy. And the Work Project doesn't provide nearly enough jobs for the people who want them. You know that, don't you?'

'Yes, sir.'

'Then why d'you want to leave?'

Mr Amory's temper was again fully evident. He hit the top of his desk with the flat of his hand. It gave a hard metallic clang.

'I want time to do other things.'

'What sort of things?'

Mr Amory leaned forward across the big desk, his heavy brows wrinkled in enquiry. Tentrix, too, was staring at him expectantly.

'Just things,' he said. 'Just private things.'

Mr Amory clapped his hands together and turned towards Tentrix. Ozzie felt that some effect of that minor explosion had caused him to return to his usual state of invisibility.

'Get down to the Filing Department and find out whatever there is to be known about it. You'll have to do it now before the interview.'

Tentrix slowly turned her head until she was staring into Mr Amory's face. Her expression was one of incredulity at being ordered about in this manner in front of someone else. There was also a flicker of malice in her eyes. For a few seconds Ozzie thought she would defy the instruction.

Mr Amory's face suddenly looked as if it had been exposed too long under the artificial sun of a lido, and Ozzie watched the dark red shadow travel down from his brow to his neck like the advancing frontier of some alarming disease. Two veins, invisible before, leaped into a

V-shaped formation in the middle of his forehead, where they glistened a vivid purple.

'Get out!' he bellowed. 'Get down to the Filing Department and find out whatever there is to know about it! And tell him about the interview! Now get out before I throw you both downstairs!'

Ozzie was terrified by this unrestrained display of temper. He'd never witnessed anything like it before, and thought it possible that Mr Amory would leap over the big desk and kill him with his bare hands. Such was his terror that he plucked at the door several times before he managed to open it.

It wasn't until he had the door open that Tentrix ceased looking at Mr Amory in her impertinent way. She caught him up in the passageway, and passed him before they reached the top of the stairs.

He looked down upon the girl's head as she descended the steep stairs in front of him. A sharp anxiety clawed at his stomach.

This small female figure swelled in his imagination until she loomed over him like a gigantic angel whose duty it was to punish forgotten sins with unimaginable pains. Her black wings beat against his heart like the pinions of some powerful machine. She was a darkly draped figure which haunted even the most cloistered recesses of his mind, hiding within its umbered folds other shapeless things.

And what was that about an interview?

She reached the bottom of the stairs, and made directly for the Filing Department without looking round. He followed unwillingly.

Mustapha was approaching along the passage. He slowed down and almost stopped, looking sideways at Tentrix with heavy eyes as she passed without acknowledging him. Ozzie had noticed often that she seemed to be incapable of walking, or making even the simplest of movements, without men staring at her. He was conscious of Mustapha, stationary now, looking back at her.

She entered the Filing Department, and Ozzie crept in after her.

Tentrix turned abruptly to face him, and he found himself looking down into her upturned face.

Prior to this he would have had great difficulty in describing her physical appearance. For him she had not so much been a person as a presence which embodied all the forces of evil which lurked in the passageways and corners of these offices and of his own mind. She had been a brooding, threatening shape, outside the range of direct vision.

But now he looked into the very features of this alien creature.

Tentrix was small, so small that she could be described as tiny. Her cheeks were rounded, and the fair hair curled over the tops of her small ears. Her brow was tall, as unwrinkled and clear as a mirror. The eyes were wide, and of a blue so faint and transparent that they might have been mere windows through which her evil spirit could look out upon the world.

She had a tiny nose. Her mouth, too, was small, like that of a child, with a short top lip and a lower lip which pouted.

But the eyes! His attention returned to her eyes. He had always thought of them as being dark, and it was a shock to discover that they were the colour of innocence and the sky. He remembered hearing that blue stars were the hottest.

'Why are you going to leave?'

It was the first time he'd heard her speak. Her voice had a sharp metallic edge.

The eyes had a frenetic and unnatural sparkle which turned their blueness into another colour from the unknown spectrum of another world. They were shameless and bold, seeming to plumb the depths of his inner world, and to rejoice in what they saw there.

'Why are you going to leave?' she repeated.

Ozzie became uncomfortable at their proximity and stepped backwards. She took a pace forward and closed the gap.

'Why?' she demanded.

'I gave the reason in Mr Amory's office.'

'What was that?'

'I said I wanted to do private things.'

She formed her lips into a circle, maintaining a hole in the middle as if she were drinking from an invisible bottle. He looked at the ring thus formed with an uneasy fascination. She put her finger in the hole and worked it sideways like a lever, so that when it came out her cheek made a soft *plop*. He wasn't sure whether this gesture was intended to convey contempt for the reason he'd given, or for Mr Amory, or both, or whether it had some quite different significance.

'Tell me about the private things you want to do,' she said, and her voice would have been a whisper if it hadn't been for its metallic edge.

'I can't. It's just that . . . well, it wouldn't be private if I told you about it, would it?'

Tentrix smiled. Her teeth were small and white, and there seemed to be too many of them in her small mouth. 'You've changed,' she said. 'You've become a different person in the last few weeks.'

'Perhaps I have.'

He hadn't thought about it in that way before, but now that he did he realized that she was probably right.

She turned away. 'Come on. Remember what Carl said.'

'Carl?'

'Carl Amory,' she said irritably. 'You've got to show me how the filing system works.'

He obediently went over to a central cabinet, which contained a number of shallow drawers.

'This is the central index,' he said, 'which you must keep up to date.'

She came to stand beside him.

'Let's say you want to find the statistics which have to do with the share of the market which each of the depots has managed to win. Depot Number One is always asking for them. You pull open this drawer and look for "M".' He acted accordingly and ran his finger along the indexed cards. 'When you find "M" you look for a card headed Market Shares, and then you . . . Hey!'

Tentrix had also run her finger along the cards and their hands came together at the required index. She caught his little finger and twisted it backwards over his knuckle until the pain made him sink to his knees.

'What are you doing?' he gasped.

Ozzie looked up at his tormentor, with his mouth stretched open by equal measures of surprise and pain. His surprise momentarily overcame his pain when he discovered that something shaped like a plum had been slipped into his mouth. He tried to swallow and almost choked. The erectile tissue stiffened and lengthened, probed the roof of his mouth, and stealthily withdrew.

He coughed and spluttered, wiping his mouth on the back of his free hand. 'Why did you do that?'

She opened her mouth very wide and put out her tongue again. The tip of it quivered and twitched up and down as if it had a life of its own. He glimpsed the soft flesh of its underside, purple and wet with saliva.

'You're funny,' she said.

She released his little finger, and he got up from the floor. He held his bruised finger in his other hand.

'I don't know what you mean about being funny.'

'You're just funny,' she repeated. 'I could have some fun with you.'

Tentrix pirouetted clockwise in the middle of the floor.

Her skirt lifted to reveal the white flesh above the tops of her stahlex knitted stockings. He stared at her, as uncomprehending a spectator as the banks of files on the surrounding shelves.

'I wouldn't let you,' he said.

She pirouetted widdershins. Her skirt lifted higher. And higher. Cold sweat broke out in the palms of his hands. He wished he were at home with his maps, he wished he were anywhere but where he actually was.

'You won't be able to stop me,' she said, coming to a stop and standing before him.

The door opened and Mustapha put his head round it. He looked quizzically at Ozzie, and then turned towards Tentrix.

'Have you told him about the interview?' he asked.

She looked at him insolently. 'No. I haven't had time yet.'

'You're a bit late then. She's here.'

Mustapha withdrew. Tentrix seemed about to say something, but then made to follow him.

'Who's here?' Ozzie asked.

'The woman who's going to interview you.'

'What about?'

But Tentrix had gone.

CHAPTER TWENTY-FOUR

'I suppose it started yesterday evening,' Jan said. 'I made some ill-informed jokes about our small son Sperry observing the First Precept. And then after breakfast this morning Sylvia dumped Sperry in the nursery and suggested that I buzz down here and reduce my ignorance.'

Arthur Medway smiled. 'While she makes her calls in Tcity. A good arrangement, and I'm grateful to Sylvia for thinking of it.'

He moved across to the drinks console. 'What would you like, Jan?'

'Thank you. Er – whisky. Malt if you have it.'

The monk's unpractised finger moved along the limited number of buttons until he identified the right one. Not surprisingly, the Vihara at Allington Castle didn't have anything like the range or diversity of the drinks kept in the cellar at Lindisfarne, or even at Hatfield.

'Does Sylvia worry about the Work Project'? he asked.

'I'm afraid she does a bit.'

Jan took the drink, wrinkled his nose and sipped. Wonderfully soft and smooth, and definitely a pure malt, although not from the Highlands. He sniffed and sipped again : a distinct peaty smell and flavour. Certainly from the Western Islands, he decided, probably from Islay.

'After all,' Jan continued, 'we are used to a no-growth, no-profit, totally planned economy, which has eliminated scarcity and want from our lives. Our management systems and enhanced intelligence enable us to manage our little planet with as much ease as an old ladies' tea party. Our work, if you can call it that, is only another pastime in our varied lives. But the effects of introducing twentieth-century working methods into the cities are difficult to predict.'

Arthur Medway, obedient to the Fifth Precept, sipped his fruit cordial. 'The only prediction you can make with any confidence is that most predictions will be wrong. It's incredible to reflect that only a couple of centuries ago people used to talk about "the death of the city" as if it were something inevitable. Developments in communications, distribution and recycling would make homes self-sufficient. Better transport would enable people to live where they wanted.'

Jan agreed: 'And so they'd all live in the country.'

'But what happened?' asked Arthur. 'Our modern cities are the biggest ever, and have a higher density of population than our forefathers dreamed of in their worst nightmares.'

Drink in hand, Jan wandered across to one of the refectory windows. The old tilting-yard, bounded by a curve of the river, echoed in his imagination with the shouts and clashing weapons of a medieval tournament.

'Not that the Citizens ever had any option,' Arthur added.

Jan rolled some more whisky round his tongue. 'We have to keep them in the cities. It's the only solution with such a large population.'

'It would nevertheless be pleasant to think they actually preferred such confinement.'

'There's some evidence that they do.'

'Really?' Arthur couldn't keep the incredulity out of his voice.

'The Central Executive has done some research on the question and Sylvia has discussed their findings with me. All of us now accept that when technology separated men from the end-product of their labours it had some bad effects; and that when automation made work unnecessary it made people lose all sense of purpose.'

'Nobody would argue with that these days,' Arthur agreed. 'For the first time in history most people had more than sufficient time to wonder what they were here for.'

'It's too early to make any statements with total confidence. But from what Sylvia has told me of the Central Executive's findings there's a good deal of evidence that the anonymous crowds in the cities give people a feeling of security.'

Arthur came over to stand beside him at the refectory window. The old tilting-yard was now a walled garden with roses and apple trees.

'A kind of brotherhood in futility,' he said.

'Brotherhood is better than isolation, Arthur.'

Arthur Medway turned towards him. Jan noticed that he had a nose which Lavater would have described as *physiognomically good*. 'There's something else that would have puzzled our ancestors. They would have been surprised that we, despite our almost limitless powers of control, should have allowed the population of Citizens to expand as it has.'

'But the answer is simple,' Jan replied. 'We allow the Citizens as much freedom as possible within their own environments. Consequently we don't interfere with their ability to have children.'

'Of course. But don't you ever wonder why they continue to have so many children despite the restricted space in which they have to live?'

Jan shrugged. 'I'll have to ask Sylvia why the Central Executive don't run a survey on the question.'

'Do you have any ideas yourself?'

'No. Do you know the answer?'

'I think so.'

Jan half-displayed, half-hid his empty glass, and was ashamed of his artifice.

'Same again?'

'Er – please. Thank you.'

Arthur took the empty glass and put it under the dispenser. 'Since the beginning of time men have yearned for immortality. Whether they admit it or not, this is the desire which is nearest to the hearts of ordinary people. And they ache for a personal immortality, not rebirth without a linking memory on the Wheel of Samsara. It is sad to think of the mountains of intellectual energy which Western man has wasted on such speculation.'

'Miguel de Unamuno,' Jan said, accepting the refilled glass.

'A perfect illustration. Then with the decline of faith men had to readjust their ways of thinking. The most positive reaction was an understanding that personal immortality isn't necessary to either happiness or virtue. Already in the twentieth century a few people had achieved this new wisdom.'

'Olaf Stapledon,' said Jan.

Arthur sipped his second fruit cordial. 'Such wisdom, which is taken for granted by the Executives, must have been very difficult to accept in those early days. The vast majority of men didn't have sufficient intellectual or moral courage. For them some alternative had to be found. The first possibility was to achieve immortality, or something like it, through creative activity. Not only could the artist make himself "immortal", he could "immortalize" other people who were otherwise not very remarkable.'

The monk, using his Executive faculty of total recall, started to give a few examples. 'Let's begin with the painters: the *condottiere* Guidoriccio was thus immortalized by Simone Martini; the son of the Strozzi family by Gentile da Fabriano; Ginevra d'Este by Pisanello; Giovanni Arnolfini and his wife by Jan van Eyck; Ranuccio Farnesi by Titian; Hélène Fourment by Rubens; Maria de Raet by van Dyck; the dwarf Sebastian de Morra by Valázquez; Monsieur Marcotte by Ingres; Mrs Graham by Gainsborough; Nelly O'Brien by Reynolds; Madame Henriot by——'

'Yes, yes,' Jan protested, alarmed lest the catalogue should be pursued until the time of Alençon.

'Or take the musical composers: the Markgraf of Brandenburg is remembered because of Bach; the violinist Clement because of Beethoven; the Haffner family because of Mozart; Harriet Smithson because of Berlioz; Dorabella because of——'

'Yes, yes,' Jan repeated, more irritably, foreseeing a series which could run as far as Raphael Rozier. These inventories from a shared *Kulturgesicht* were all very well when they were used for private meditation, but they could become a very plague in conversation.

'And in literature,' Arthur continued. 'We remember

Laurette de Noves because of Petrarch; Penelope Devereux because of Philip Sidney; Lucy Sacheverell because of Richard Lovelace; Edward King because of Milton; Mary Temple because of——'

Jan raised his hand in a final protest. '*Please*, Arthur, you have made your point and let me conclude it :

So long as men can breathe, or eyes can see,
So long lives this, and this gives life to thee.'

Arthur Medway smiled his acceptance of the rebuke. 'Such an alternative, either as creator or as re-created, was never available to more than a tiny minority. After the Denaissance, when the creative impulse died, it ceased to be available to anyone. The other alternative remained, although I'm sure it isn't recognized for what it really is.'

Jan concluded the point again with a couplet from the same source :

'*And nothing 'gainst Time's scythe can make defence*
Save breed, to brave him when he takes thee hence.'

'And if one candle is lighted from another,' said the monk, 'who can say that the light of the second isn't the same light as the first?'

Jan finished his whisky and put it on the console.

Arthur gestured towards a trestle table. 'Should we sit down?'

Jan pulled a chair up to the table, and saw that the stahlex top had been treated to resemble a coarse-grained wood. He ran his fingers across the simulated adze-marks with admiration.

'I'm afraid that you'll find our dinners here rather frugal.'

The food comprised nothing but cheese, fruit and nuts. Inspection of the enormous cheese board, however, showed that it contained a variety of soft cheeses, French blue mould cheeses, genuine Swiss Gruyère and Emmenthal, American Edam, Trappist cheeses from the abbeys of Normandy and Burgundy, as well as other varieties which Jan didn't recognize.

'On the contrary,' Jan said, cutting a piece of Soumaintrain and peeling off the orange rind. 'You do very well for someone whose rules forbid him to eat after noon.'

Arthur cracked a walnut. 'Buddhas only point the way. That particular rule was a good one, but it's inappropriate to Western man because of our colder climate. Respect for our health obliges us to have a medicine meal in the evening.'

There was a clapping of wings. A brown pigeon landed outside the refectory window, immediately followed by a wooing cock bird. Another clap of wings and they both disappeared.

The incident reminded Jan of their interrupted conversation in the courtyard. 'You were going to say something about the brown pigeons before we came inside.'

'Yes, I was.' He concentrated for a moment on carefully splitting another walnut with the pair of stahlex nutcrackers. 'I was going to say that in times gone by people took pleasure in reflecting that the pigeons were dressed in the same brown as the Carmelite monks who had a foundation here in Allington Castle. Now the brown habits of the Carmelites have been replaced by the saffron robes of the Bhikkhus. Some things change, but other things remain the same. The brown pigeons, which Wyatt brought with the sonnet from Italy, remind us that the effects of the Renaissance are still with us.'

'In what way?' Jan broached another cheese with a reddish crust, and lightly pressed a section between finger and thumb until it bulged slightly:

'Sus! qu'à plein gosier on s'écrie:
Bény soit le territoire de Brie.

Pont-l'Evêque, arrière de nous!
Auvergne et Milan, cachez-vous.'

Arthur extracted the nut from its fractured shell, and poured some wine from a carafe into Jan's glass. He poured himself a tumbler of water.

'Wyatt was the archetypal Renaissance man,' he continued. 'He was one of the "new company of courtly makers". In the cities of Italy to which he was sent on diplomatic missions he absorbed the spirit of what seemed to be a human rebirth. He was tall, handsome, dextrous in the use of arms, generous and honourable, fluent in foreign languages, a fine singer who accompanied himself on the lute. He embodied the new spirit of delight in life and all that it can offer. It seemed as if we were only a little lower than the gods in our capacity to understand and enjoy the beauties of this world. Never had men's eyes been so fired by the beauty of what they saw.' He popped the nut into his mouth. 'This endless craving of the senses, this thirst to experience all the sensual pleasures of life, is comprehended by the Pali word *tanha*.'

'We are all indebted to Sir Thomas and his kind,' Jan said. He sipped the wine, and rolled it against the back of his teeth. 'The veritable flavour of the Pinot Chardonnay.'

'From the San Joaquin valley, however. Not from Chablis.' Arthur cracked another walnut and eased it from its shell. 'In the Fire Sermon which Buddha preached at Uruvela, he explained how all the impressions received by our eyes are on fire. Everything burns with the fires of lust and illusion. We can be truly happy only if we turn our backs on these fires. We must reject *tanha* if we are to escape from the cause of our sorrow and the Wheel of Samsara, the circle of life and death which turns for ever.'

Jan swirled the wine in his glass. 'We have inherited the brown pigeons from the Renaissance. It is our duty to cherish them. But you suggest we ameliorate matters by feeding them with Indian corn.'

'They will persist in being the same brown pigeons, nevertheless.'

Arthur Medway flipped the nut into his mouth and refilled Jan's glass.

'You seem determined to make me feel the irony of the situation,' Jan said, swigging the wine and pushing his chair back from the table.

Arthur made a hidden gesture and a humidor arose in the centre of the table, shaped in the form of a *Stupa* or burial ground for relics of the Buddha. The lid opened to reveal a cedar-lined box containing cigars. Jan selected one. As he removed the band he saw that it said *Elaborados a mano.*

'I am glad you feel the irony,' Arthur said. 'I am frequently aware of it in my own position.'

Jan lit the cigar and puffed contentedly. It had been a good meal. 'In what way?'

'My head is shaved according to the custom of the Vihara. But that makes me indistinguishable from the millions of men in the cities who use depilatories because they can't afford to visit a barber. I am allowed three robes of the cheapest cotton. In fact I wear a robe of knitted stahlex which will last for ever. My only other possessions should be a razor, a water-strainer and a needle. But I use depilatory cream like everybody else, and have no need of the other three items. And what, my dear Jan, would you put in my begging-bowl if I presented you with it? I am sworn to poverty, but I'm surrounded by Executive privileges which couldn't have been purchased with the wealth of Asoka's empire.'

Jan pondered a moment, drawing slowly on his cigar. 'It's just as well that Buddhas only point the way.'

Arthur Medway laughed. This was only the second time his amusement had become audible. It was the peaceful, inward smile that Jan was going to remember.

When Jan finally took his leave, the monk followed him out to the gatehouse. He again felt the firm handshake, with the brief extra pressure which seemed to transmit something of its own steadfast assurance.

He turned to wave a last farewell as the auto rolled away on the gravelled drive. The elderly monk looked very tall and straight as he stood in the shadows of the gateway, slowly waving. Jan imagined that he could still see the quiet inward smile.

CHAPTER TWENTY-FIVE

Gloriana Schnurrbush was transfixed. She couldn't have been more paralysed if the joints of her old bones had finally locked together.

'Look!' she whispered. 'Look there!'

Dab crawled across the floor towards her, dragging his maimed back leg behind him. He thrust his chin on to her bony knee, and rolled his brown eyes upwards to look into her face.

'No!' she said. 'Over there! Look! Over there!'

The handle inside the outer door had rotated, as if being turned by an invisible hand. It remained in that position for a moment, and then sprang back to its original location. Then it rotated again.

'It's a ghost, Dab!'

The handle again returned to its first location. But now the invisible hand became impatient, and twisted the handle violently several times. After that it desisted. The handle returned to its initial position and didn't move any more.

'Of course it's not a ghost. Don't be silly, Dab! It's someone trying to get in from outside.'

Gloriana's brittle legs straightened, and Dab slithered

backwards on his deformed legs. She took a tottering step towards the door, and then another one; a pause while she regained her balance; then another step; and another one. Dab crawled behind her.

'It's my Steve!' she croaked. 'It's my Steve come back to me after all these years. I should have known as soon as I saw the handle going up and down. It's Steve! Up and down,' she repeated.

Her progress was slow and painful. Dab followed with his nose against her creaking ankle-bones.

'Steve! Steve! I'm coming, Steve!'

Gloriana tried to shout more loudly, but the extra effort stopped any noise coming out at all. She finally reached the door, and turned the handle in her arthritic fingers. The door opened.

'It's Bushy,' she cried. 'It's your very own Bushy.'

For the first time in many years Gloriana Schnurrbush looked out into vestibule 333.

Nothing had changed. It was full of people, people, people, marching past like mechanical toys which were being continuously manufactured by some ingenious machine at the other end of the vestibule. They were marching, marching, marching towards corridor 18, with empty faces and unfocused eyes, just as they always had. Everything was still the same, same, same.

No. Something had changed. She directed her eyes to a bright metallic surface, which showed where the ring of the door handle used to be. Why on earth should...

There was a dog in the corridor. It was proceeding with difficulty because of a malformation in its hind limbs, but it soon disappeared among those hundreds of marching legs.

'Dab!' she squawked. 'Don't leave me, Dab!'

Gloriana hobbled out into the vestibule, where the first accidental kick caused her to subside like a wigwam with a broken pole.

CHAPTER TWENTY-SIX

Taggart, on his way home to his module in the First Sector, discovered that the dense crowd of which he was a particle had developed into some species of whirlpool. He'd noticed this phenomenon before in the corridors. It appeared to happen when a sufficient number of pedestrians were trying to turn off from the main stream, while the majority wished to go straight on.

After some effort to direct his own course he gave in to the prevailing movement, and was carried round and round in a circle like a lost bird. He drifted about until he bobbed up against an open doorway. A resurgence of pressure behind floated him inside to a darkened room.

He experienced the dizzying sensation of being completely lost on an unknown sea, without the faintest glimmer of a distant beacon to guide him. It was a kind of consummation. He'd been lost ever since he'd seen his mother asleep, with the delicate pink tracery on her back.

Taggart relived the time of his apocalypse.

The white flesh was criss-crossed with thick purple ridges, which looked as if they could have been a substance squeezed out of a tube, or as if they were long glistening worms. Within the interstices of this swollen network there was another random pattern, dull red and less pronounced; and within the remaining spaces there were fainter lines, pink and soft; and between and beneath these marks there was an infinitely complex web of a myriad other lines, fading through their spectrum of pain from purple to pink, until they died into the whiteness from which they had been born.

He had been lost ever since that day.

Now that his eyes had accommodated to the darkness he saw that he was in a long room, with a dimly illuminated shrine or figure at the other end. When he walked forward he became aware of an area of more intense darkness above his head, and looking up he saw a circle of blackness where the ceiling had been sucked up into the underside of a dome. The side walls of the room were heavily embossed with pyramidal frames, beneath which brightly coloured pictures appeared from time to time.

Taggart approached the first picture, which disappeared before he reached it. When he was within a couple of strides the picture reappeared under its pagoda roof, and at the same time he must have entered an acoustic shield and triggered a recorded commentary. The singsong voice, slightly reminiscent of the Sixth Sector, greeted him cordially:

'Good morning, afternoon or evening. This first picture shows our Lord's first act of mercy. Here you see Prince Siddârtha anointing a wound in the wing of a swan.'

He looked at the animated picture and listened to the commentary. The central figure was a brown-skinned man, who sat cross-legged throughout the sequence and at the end laid the swan's neck against his smooth cheek.

The picture blacked out, and Taggart moved on.

The next picture came to life under its pagoda frame. Again he looked at the brown-skinned, cross-legged man. The singsong voice explained:

'This is Prince Siddârtha's first meditation. Our Lord, who hitherto had seen nothing but the superficial beauties of existence, is meditating under a jambu tree.'

The following picture showed the same man weeping silent tears as he left a beautiful girl asleep with a baby at her breast. The voice within the acoustic shield spoke in softer tones:

'Prince Siddârtha is taking leave of Yasôdhara, the wife whom he had loved in previous lives as both man and beast.'

Another picture showed the Prince sitting under an unfading Bôdhi tree, where he was subjected to a variety of temptations by devils. Taggart's interest waxed temporarily when the devils assumed female forms. But he remembered another face, with rounded cheeks and fair hair curling forward over small ears. The singsong voice ended this recitation by talking about the triumph of good over evil, and Taggart moved on.

The next couple of pictures contained the moving forms of tigers. The first showed the lair of a starving tigress with cubs pulling at her empty teats. The Prince entered and threw himself down in front of the tigress. She was too weak to take advantage of the meal, until he cut his throat and induced her to start feeding. The next picture showed Yasôdhara coming forward to greet her future husband wearing a veil of black and gold. This was to show that she remembered his fierce love centuries ago, when they were both tigers in the forest.

Taggart turned to leave. Unwittingly he entered the confines of another acoustic shield, and triggered another recording.

'That young Prince became Buddha. He searched for the answer to the most important question that a man can ask.'

Annoyed by this further intrusion, Taggart turned round with the intention of heading directly for the exit. But the next words stopped him.

'Buddhahood dwells within you, also. You too can avoid suffering.'

He hesitated. The woman who'd interviewed him had said something about Buddha.

He discovered that he was now in front of the shrine which he'd noticed when he first entered the temple. He saw that it was the seated figure of a man, made from burnished stahlex which glowed under some hidden source of light. The head was square-shaped, with a bob of hair above the centre of the skull, and something which looked like a third eye in the middle of a wide, low forehead. The eyelids were thick, lowered, covering eyes which looked upon something other than the external world. The lips were full and slightly curved, as if at any moment they would spread into a smile.

'Are you unhappy? Do you feel that you have been made to suffer without just cause? Have you ever seen someone you loved suffer unhappiness through no fault of their own? Do you sometimes think that if there is a god, then he must be a devil?'

Taggart's lips formed the word 'Yes' but no sound issued from them.

'Of course you sometimes feel like this. If you didn't, you yourself would be some kind of devil. But the Buddha has explained it all.'

He looked at the seated figure. It was at peace with the world, despite the unnatural position of its limbs; the legs were crossed in an awkward way; one hand lay in its lap, and the fingers of the other hand pointed upward as if to that other world which was visible to its veiled eyes.

'Natural justice does prevail despite appearances to the contrary. If you see a wicked person, who appears to be happy in his wickedness, you can be sure that he'll be unhappy in the future.'

'It's not true,' Taggart whispered. His father had never been punished, neither for the way he'd treated his mother, nor for sending him to the crèche in the First Sector.

'All the unhappiness you see in the world is the result of previous wickedness.'

'It's not true!' he shouted. 'It's just not true!'

'You may say you've known someone who had led an absolutely blameless life, as blameless as an angel, and who was nevertheless inflicted with some terrible punishment.'

Taggart nodded.

'Or you may say that you've known someone who did evil things, who inflicted suffering upon others much better than himself, and who was never punished.'

He nodded again, more vigorously.

'That is why the doctrine of Karma is inevitably linked with the doctrine of rebirth. If a man doesn't suffer for his evil deeds in this life, he will suffer for them in another reincarnation.'

Taggart, who had been listening intently, shook his head. It was a trick. It was nothing but words. It was all rubbish.

'For many centuries one third of the world's population has accepted the doctrine of reincarnation as being self-evident, and not even open to doubt.'

Taggart looked at the dreaming, golden eyelids, and the wide mouth which was trying not to broaden into a grin. It was a joke. The whole thing was a joke. One-third of the world's population had always been wrong. Inheritance from grandparents, or from an unknown father, or something of that sort, explained the other things the voice went on to talk about.

'The true number of poets, scientists, and philosophers who have existed is only a tiny fraction of those who are remembered under different names.

'Why has creative activity dwindled and disappeared over the last couple of centuries? Because Raphael Rozier and Alençon were among the last of the creative spirits to escape from the Wheel of Samsara, which is the ever-turning wheel of pain, death and rebirth.'

That was wrong, too. Creative people had disappeared because their functions had been taken over by computers. Everybody knew that. Computers wrote poems, drew pictures——

'If your brain has not already given you proof that you have previously existed then you're in a very small minority. Let me explain.'

Taggart, who had become restless and was again on the point of leaving, hesitated once more. Proof that he'd already existed in other bodies!

'Have you ever gone somewhere for the first time in your life, and yet been unable to rid yourself of the conviction that you'd been there before?'

He tensed. Only this morning, when he entered the saloon for that interview, he had lived through such an experience. The unexpected sense of familiarity had been so strong that he'd blurted something about it to the strange woman whose head curved outwards above her ears.

'Have you ever met anyone whom you immediately disliked?'

Yes, he had. Mr Felixtowe, for instance. But his dislike of Mr Felixtowe was as nothing compared to the hatred of his father.

'And have you ever met anyone with whom you immediately became firm friends? Someone you instinctively knew you could trust?'

No, not really. Although he could have have trusted the strange woman who had interviewed him in the saloon. He had known that she wanted to help him.

'And what about "love at first sight"? How often do a man and woman meet, and know that they are "made for each other"? As soon as they begin to talk they discover that they "have everything in common". They see the truth of the situation in each other's eyes.'

Taggart had fewer reflections on this part of the argument. He'd never fallen in love with a girl, at first sight or otherwise. His mother had been little more than a girl.

'There can be only one explanation for these sudden relationships. The person whom you instinctively distrust is someone who betrayed you in a previous life. The immediate friendship is for someone who helped you in an earlier existence. The spontaneous love is for someone whom you loved in a different body.'

If he ever met a girl with eyes of a certain blue, with hair curling forward over her ears, might she remember the songs she used to sing and which he had forgotten? Would she remember how she had been flayed before an audience with a stahlex whip? Would she understand his love and his hatred?

> *'All life is one, and everything that lives or waits to be born is part of the same life. We know that many centuries ago our Lord Buddha lived in the body of a tiger. When you see a wicked man who is happy, remember that when you next see him he might be in the skin of some wretched animal.'*

Taggart was silent for a while, and then a short laugh hiccupped in his throat. The whole thing was preposterous. Now he did finally turn away, ignoring the pictures on the other wall, and made his way directly towards the exit. He must have been mad to listen for so long to that singsong voice.

The absurdity of the proposition grew upon him, and he was chortling to himself as he reached the exit. A man suffering for his previous sins in the skin of some wretched animal! He was laughing so much that he didn't pay full attention to where he was putting his feet, and he stumbled over a dog as he entered the corridor.

The dog looked up at him with big brown eyes. Taggart recovered his balance, and the dog began to scurry away.

The dog couldn't move away as quickly as it wanted, because there was something the matter with its hind legs. The left leg had been maimed, so that it was permanently cranked and dragged along behind the other one. This jerking progress was accompanied by a scraping noise, as the claws of the dead foot scraped along the ground.

'Dad?' he gasped.

The animal stopped immediately, and looked round. It wagged its tail limply, and looked up at him. The big brown eyes were set in a long face. There was no doubt about it.

'Dad! Dad!'

Taggart sprang forward, and seized the dog by the scruff of its neck.

'Forgive me, Lord Buddha,' he begged happily, 'for having doubted your doctrine.'

CHAPTER TWENTY-SEVEN

Osbert Osborne was glad to get away from the office and escape from the woman with the oddly shaped head. She had put an extraordinary series of questions to him, many of which seemed to imply that he had overlooked some very good reason for continuing to work: if not at Tcity Consultants, then somewhere else. He had ended by sullenly repeating that he had something more important to do, and stubbornly refusing to say what it was.

As soon as he was free he chose, as always, an alternative route home to his module. For the first time, as he thought, he entered vestibule 333. He was on his way to corridor 18 when he saw it.

Ozzie was like a man who, after long absence and experiences in distant places, returns to the scenes of a happy childhood. The man identifies himself in the child that was, and discovers that what he has become is what he always had been.

The quest had ended.

It seemed long, long, long ago when that handle had opened an invisible door that showed him another universe which was so much larger, brighter, richer than the one he had been living in. It was in this vestibule, outside this very door, that he'd been reborn into a life which had a meaning, a pattern, a new dimension that he could never have imagined. It was on this very spot that, without knowing it, he had truly become himself.

And yet it was only a few weeks ago. His heart ached with gratitude as he took out the tube of Meltstahl. In his impatience his hand shook, and he began to twist the handle before he had properly applied the nozzle.

CHAPTER TWENTY-EIGHT

Will Forstell knew that he was as strong as any number of elephants, whether of the divine incense-exhaling variety or not, when he left Vajra-Yogini.

He made his way on to the fast lane on the northbound paveline in Thruway 1. On the southbound line, going in the opposite direction, he saw a dog. It was a woebegone creature, sitting awkwardly as if there were something the matter with its legs. As he passed the animal gazed at him with uncomprehending eyes which seemed to ask why it should be forced to expiate sins beyond its comprehension.

The dog was obviously lost. Like most people, Will thought. They don't know where they are, where they're going, or what they want to do.

But he knew where he was going.

He side-tracked, stepped on to the sidewalk, and turned off to follow a sign which directed him to the Autoterminus. He felt as if he could have vaulted the barrier if he'd wanted to, and he crossed the compound with springs under his heels. The stahlex trees with their welded frames were natural outgrowths of his own joy in living.

The Reception Area was crowded. Some of the people were on their way home after an evening's pleasure in the

First Sector. Others, less languorous, were about to go across. Many were doing neither, and had come to enjoy by association the pleasures of those who could afford such things.

Will noticed somebody with a pink drink in a narrow-stemmed glass. He went over to a vending machine, scanned the pictures, and found what he wanted. The drink was slightly acid, with bubbles that prickled his nose and made his eyes water.

He walked up and down the Reception Area, sipping from the narrow-stemmed glass and reliving his memories of Vagini, the Tibetan priestess or whatever she was. That Buddhism thing had certainly put him on the right path. He felt like a million divine incense-exhaling elephants.

Will threw his empty glass into a disposal chute and sauntered over to the ticket dispensers which ran the full length of one wall. After one short, ambiguous step, he went to the dispenser furthest to the right. Without lowering his eyes to read the hire-cost he inserted his credit card in the scanning slot. For a second some part of his mind hoped that the credit wouldn't be allowed.

But those weeks at home had brought their reward. There was a brief whirring noise, and a silver ticket popped into his hand. With a swinging step he descended the stahlex steps to the departure bay.

The auto was even longer, even more glittering, with even larger tail fins, and altogether more like a spaceship than he'd imagined. As soon as he sat in it the instructions in *How To Drive An Auto* entered his mind without any conscious effort to recall them.

He pressed the green button, released the handbrake, and the auto slid away into an exit tunnel where the ceiling lights lit up and switched off to chart its progress. The advice contained in *The New Autocomplex* came unbidden to his mind. He slowed down, and eased his way on to the ring road.

Once established there, he cut his way like a knife through the intervening traffic and entered the first radial road to the traffic circle. And as soon as he was on the traffic circle he really began to enjoy himself. *Tra-la-la-lalala-la-la.*

He used his horn and headlights as if they were some species of advanced weaponry, and the vehicles in front melted away like snow. He found the exit he wanted for the Second Sector without difficulty, but changed his mind and turned off to complete a few more circuits of the ring road. *Tra-la-la.*

A small, squarish black car was in his path. Will switched his lights on-and-off, on-and-off, and kept his horn blaring until the route was clear. *Tra-la-la.*

This was what life was about – *lalala-la-la.* When that woman came to interview him tomorrow about the Work Project, he knew what he'd tell her. The Work Project was a success. A complete success. That ought to please her.

Another black box on wheels was in his path. But not for long.

Tra-la-la. Tra-la-la-lalala-la-la. Tra-la-la. Tra-la-la . . .

CHAPTER TWENTY-NINE

Taggart first saw her on the northbound paveline in Thruway 1.

It was only a back view, but there was something about the posture of the small head, the set of the shoulders, which created a yawning sense of emptiness beneath his ribs. He was aware of his heart beating painfully in vacancy, like a heavy clapper in a large brass bell.

She was obscured for a moment by the crowd, and then reappeared as she side-tracked into the slow lane. He followed.

There was something, too, about the way her quick feet moved in front of each other once she was on the sidewalk. He hurried after her, frantic with anxiety lest he should lose track of her. At the first side-street she left the thruway. He drew alongside her in the mob which was trying to squeeze through the beeblock doorway.

It was true!

Taggart looked down at the round face, with the fair hair curling over the tops of her small ears; at the tall, smooth brow; at the wide, almost transparent eyes; at the childlike pouting mouth.

'I've found you,' he said, taking her gently by the arm.

She shook his hand off.

'Who do you think you are?'

'Don't you know?' he asked.

'Should I?'

He thought hard. 'Perhaps not. But I know who you are. Who you really are.'

They were halfway through the doorway now. He worked vigorously with his elbows to keep his place beside her. A concerted shove from behind thrust them into the corridor.

'Come with me,' he begged.

'Where?'

'My module.'

She laughed, showing small, white teeth. 'You don't waste much time. Does it work with other girls?'

'I'm not interested in . . . in other girls. You're the first one I've ever spoken to.'

She laughed again, looking into his eyes and crowing with disbelief, but didn't remove his hand this time. He glanced at the electroluminous ceiling indicators, and guided her into the correct lane for the levator station. The levator door clashed behind them, and the unlit chamber climbed up its shaft like a rocket.

Taggart would have liked the journey to last for ever. He was destined for those stars which glimmered in the narrow spaces above the thruways. To stand in the darkness, with his hand on her arm, feeling the warmth of her body against his side, made him dizzy with disbelief at his good fortune; and to know that her round bright face was almost against his shoulder, was not to travel in darkness at all.

The chamber stopped abruptly and they were thrown out into the next corridor.

'This is silly,' she said. 'I don't know anything about you.'

'You'll soon start to remember.'

'What do you mean?' She stopped to demand an explanation, but the crowd behind swept them forwards. 'Why should I go with you?'

Taggart looked down into her upturned face, was aware of her eyes looking questioningly into his. 'Because you must,' he said. 'Because you *must*.'

He steered her into the vestibule where he lived, keeping tight hold of her arm. Quickly he opened his module door, terrified that she would change her mind, that she was teasing him, and that she would escape at the last moment. He pushed her inside, stepped in after her, and leaned with his back against the closed door.

Taggart closed his eyes. In the perfect silence of the module he was bereft of sensation, floating in the still air. When he spoke his voice was a weary exhalation, the echo of a half-forgotten memory, issuing from some bodiless mouth above his head.

'Sing to me.'

He opened his eyes. She was laughing soundlessly. 'Sing to me,' he repeated.

She moved towards him.

'Let me out of here. I've had enough of this stupid game.'

Taggart set the lock on the door, came forward, and struck her violently on the shoulder. She spun round under the impact, hit the wall, and almost fell to the floor. He stood over her with his hand raised. She was now staring at him with a curious expression on her face, a mixture of amusement and apprehension.

'Sing!' he shouted. 'Sing! Sing! Sing!'

Her mouth trembled as she spoke. 'What do you want me to sing?'

'You know the songs!'

She slithered away from beneath the threatening hand and stood at the other end of the tiny cubicle. Her eyes were on his face and he saw the growing fear in them.

'Sing! Sing! Sing! Sing!'

His voice cracked and broke. She started to sing in a wobbly, uncertain voice.

'You see them here,
You see them there,
You see them almost everywhere.
In vestibule,
In each module,
The products of the Stahlex Corpora-a-ation.'

'That's not it!' he bawled. 'Think! Think! Remember one of the songs you used to sing!'

She persevered with the next verse. He thought he could see a look of despair in her eyes. Her voice, instead of growing strong, became less assured as she progressed.

'You see them high,
You see them low,
You see them everywhere you go.

In corridor,
On every door,
The products of the Stahlex Corpora-a-ation.'

'I'll make you remember!' he screamed, tearing at a sliding cupboard in the wall. He thrust his hand inside and started clawing about in search of something.

'You see them far,
You see them wide,
You see them everywhere beside.
In beeblock walls,
And watchmacalls,
The products of the Stahlex Corpora-a-a-a-ation.'

She finished on a high, quavering note, and was trying to prolong it as much as possible while she searched her memory for another tri-di advertising jingle. Her voice faded and died when she saw what he was holding in his hand. The handle was black and shiny, and the thong was woven out of stahlex thread.

Taggart ignored her, however, and threw open the door to the sleeping-cubicle.

'Dad!' he yelled. 'Come on, Dad! I've got another surprise for you.'

The dog dragged itself out, trailing its hind legs. A damp, warm, sickly smell pervaded the room. The dog's hair didn't grow all over it properly and there were bald, pink spots here and there. The animal looked up at Taggart with large, brown eyes.

'There she is, Dad. Remember her, don't you, Dad?'

Taggart started to flog the creature with demented energy, driving it round and round in a circle which had the girl at its centre.

'Sing! Sing!' he panted.

Her memory was inspired.

'Stahlex threads
Are good for beds
And other things besides.
In shining gleams
Of knicker seams
Another use resides.'

For the moment he was more preoccupied with the dog than with her. She knew another two verses, and hoped that might be sufficient. With one eye on the lock of the door she began the second verse, and began to edge away.

CHAPTER THIRTY

Osbert Osborne's first day of total freedom was unsatisfying in a way that frightened him. It almost seemed a pity that he should have found the ring on coming home after his last day at the office of Tcity Consultants. It would somehow have been better if he'd been forced to spend several weeks or months, or even years, in the quest.

There was still the endless search for other items for his collection. That would go on indefinitely, he reminded himself, as he opened his module door. But today, at least, there hadn't been the old excitement in his explorations.

It was now that he became aware of a small figure behind him. The struggle was a short one.

'I told you that you wouldn't be able to stop me,' Tentrix said, as she entered the living-cubicle.

Ozzie unfolded two seats from the wall and thumbed the dispenser for a couple of synthetic beers. She went straight to the tri-di and fiddled with the buttons until she found the channel she wanted.

Princess Oriana was practising her usual ablutions in the gilded scallop shell.

The Princess didn't notice the moving shadows at the window; or if she did, she must have thought they were cast by the branches of the cedars in the palace garden. A camera moved in to focus upon the climbing limbs of what appeared to be a giant red caterpillar, but which was really an alien from the second planet of Epsilon Eridani. The monster inserted a leg through a partly-opened casement and its horny integument made a screeching noise on the glass.

Princess Oriana looked up and screamed. And screamed.

Ozzie, having failed to draw Tentrix's attention to the cans of beer, sat in the other seat with both drinks beside him.

The creature now had the casement fully open, and began to pour its long length into the room, joint after glistening joint, as leg after leg scrambled over the window frame. Oriana stood up in her scallop shell with her hands raised to her mouth in terror, a soapy Venus newborn from the cleansing waters.

The red caterpillar was almost fully into the room, but it kept its back end in the open casement, anchoring itself there with a couple of pairs of hind legs. It reared up on its stomach and revealed a supple torso, made up of segments and given flexibility by a series of mucous rings. A dozen pairs of legs snatched the Princess from her gilded bath and pressed her against the warty chest. She herself looked like a small white insect imprisoned in a many-barred cage.

Ozzie drank some beer. No matter how the programme developed, it was a welcome interlude before whatever Tentrix might have in mind.

The monster retreated backwards the way it had come with Oriana tightly enfolded in its forward pairs of legs.

The room was emptied, and only a trail of soapsuds on the floor and glutinous streaks around the window frame showed that Oriana's toilet had again suffered an interruption.

Ozzie observed the stiffness of Tentrix's shoulders. So entranced was she by this encounter that she was scarcely breathing. He drank some more beer.

The cameras followed the absconding creature under the low branches of the cedars, out of the palace gardens, and into the pleasant woodland beyond. The monster halted in a grassy glade, beneath some ancient elms, tall and straight. It tried to force mandibular kisses upon the screaming Princess, but succeeded in doing little more than leave viscous trails along her twisting neck.

Tentrix wriggled forward on to the edge of her seat, her eyes focused on the drama with unwinking intensity. What could be the matter with her? It was only another variation on the same old endless theme, reflected Ozzie, as he finished the first can of beer.

The native from the second planet of Epsilon Eridani became impatient, and adopted more direct tactics. It poked Oriana about, to make quite sure she was still the right way round, and began to transfer her backwards along its underside by a kind of external peristalsis. The legs behind her moved forward a pair at a time to seize her bare ankles, pulled her along under the glistening torso, and then moved forward again to grip her legs above the knee. With each regression a fresh pair of legs came into play, seizing first the ankles and then the thighs, with the precise timing of an automatic machine. Meanwhile the upper pairs of legs, working in phase with the lower pairs, kept pushing her downwards by her shoulders.

Thus Princess Oriana pursued her backward course along the underside of the red caterpillar. The concerted movements of all those legs made it look as if she were imprisoned behind the bars of a moving grille.

Tentrix slid from the seat on to her knees, and watched

the action on all fours. Ozzie opened the second stahlex can.

Oriana had now left the warty chest, and was being pulled across a white expanse of belly. This area of the creature's underside was soft, and in her struggles her elbows and knees made indentations in it, as if in a large comfortable bed. The additional pairs of hinder legs which came into play began to move faster, forwards and backwards, forwards and backwards, with ever increasing speed. The ringed body of the red caterpillar was exuding its fluids in larger quantities, so that the body of the Princess was covered in a white slime. This caused the legs to slip and lose their grip upon her shining limbs. The busy legs moved even faster, but maintained equal acceleration at both top and bottom, and remained perfectly in phase as each pair of legs took over from each preceding pair.

Princess Oriana, completely exhausted, ceased to struggle. The giant red caterpillar rolled over on its back, so that the last pairs of legs could work without impediment. The Princess, face downwards on the lower part of the quaking white belly, was inexorably being moved along to the monster's nether regions. Her screams, which had become weaker and weaker until they disappeared, suddenly recommenced with greater force than before.

Tentrix crawled towards the screen until she was almost part of the action. Ozzie finished the second can of beer, and went into the sleeping-cubicle.

He looked at his collection.

Each item had a label attached, giving the number of the vestibule, the nearest corridor, and the floor on which it was found. Each label was a flag which signalled the high point of an adventure. Some day, he hoped, he would need to go over all these labels again, and add *Aidan, Fourth Sector*; because some day, at a distance in time that he couldn't calculate, he would begin to explore the other beeblocks in this sector – Cuthbert, Oswald, and all the others – and then the other sectors.

Princess Oriana's screams subsided into sobs.

What was the matter with people? There must be something fundamentally wrong with them, or they wouldn't behave the way they did. Something *really* wrong with them. Some piece of the jigsaw must have been lost, or cut to the wrong shape.

Oriana's sobs declined into groans.

It was a simple matter, really. All you had to do was find out what you liked doing, and do it. With ordinary luck, and a little patience, you would find out what it was you wanted to do before very long. What he would most like to do at this very moment would be to sit down with his maps and crayon those new vestibules and corridors that he'd covered today, fruitless though the adventure had been. Then he would like to sit and brood over them, and decide upon the routes he should take tomorrow.

A wild yell came from the next room.

Coonan, he decided, and returned to the living-cubicle.

It was indeed Coonan, the barbarian king. A lethal flame lit his eyes, the veins on his temples knotted, and his features convulsed with a fury terrible to behold as he raged to the rescue of the ravaged Princess. His head was thrust forward on his corded neck, and as he swung his heavy sword he revealed the countless fighting scars that criss-crossed his mighty frame.

Chunks of severed caterpillar began to fly about in the air. Even after the head was severed some parts of the torso retained sufficient life, or the effects of life, to incommode Oriana painfully.

'Oh, my lord!' she sobbed, and threw her arms around his neck in a frenzied embrace.

Coonan grunted and took her in his sinewy arms. The allegro from Raphael Rozier's 213th Symphony (electro-whistle and snare drums) echoed through the leafy glade.

Tentrix, looking like a third figure in the tri-di projection, immediately lost interest and stood up. She blanked the screen and turned to Ozzie. Her face was flushed.

'Hey!' she said. 'Did you see that old snake?'

He looked round quickly. 'No. Where?'

'On the tri-di. That old snake thing with all those legs. You must have seen it.'

'Oh that! Yes.' He nodded vigorously to make up for having been so slow.

'But I liked the one with the ant men better,' she said. 'Didn't you?'

Ozzie went about it tentatively. 'A snake thing with ant men?'

'No! Why don't you listen? The ant men came up out of the plughole in that shell thing while she was having her bath. Don't you remember?'

He was apologetic. 'I think I must have missed it,' he confessed, although he had missed nearly all of them except the one he'd just seen; and what he'd seen had convinced him that if you missed them all you missed one.

'You can't have missed it,' she argued. 'They kept coming up through the plughole and eating her. They kept eating her until Coonan rushed in and sprayed them with some special stuff.'

'Sorry. I must've missed it.'

'Then he swilled them down the plughole,' she added, as if this final circumstance might jog his obstinate memory.

'Sorry.'

Tentrix came towards him, and raised her hands to his shoulders as if to hold him steady while she aimed the blue bullets in her eyes. He had the odd sensation of looking into her eyes and out through the back of her head. She raised her hands, seized the almost nonexistent lobes of his ears, and pulled his face downwards until their noses were touching.

'You're hurting me again,' he said.

Her face was too near for him to focus on more than two or three features, separately, and without any precision. He saw one eye, glazed with pale blue ice; a section of a small ear. They seemed like parts of different women.

'I'm going to have some fun with you,' she said.

'How d'you know?'

'Because you're different.'

The pain in his ears increased, and was then obliterated by a sharper sensation in his bottom lip. He twisted his head, and saw the frozen blue light in her other eye. He floundered like a fish, hooked irretrievably through the lip with the barb inside its mouth. She backed away, and he tasted sweetness.

'I don't know what you mean by fun,' he said.

She began to undo the stahlex buttons at her throat. 'All people are different, and some of them are funny. Sometimes I think all of them are funny, in their different ways. Yesterday I met this man in the First Sector. He had staring eyes and pleaded with me to go home with him.'

Ozzie looked at her rounded cheeks, and the fair hair curling over the tops of her small ears; her wide, light blue eyes; her childish mouth. It was conceivable, he supposed, that there might be people mad enough to plead with her to go home with them.

'When we got back to his module he wanted me to sing.' She laughed. 'I didn't mind that so much, until I found out about the dog.'

'Which dog?'

'The one I'm telling you about. It had kind of bald spots. When I looked more closely I could see that the skin was swollen and cut open.'

Ozzie licked his bottom lip. The sweet taste was still there. Tentrix ran her thumb through the remaining buttons on the top half of her dress, and wrinkled her nose.

'Not that I wanted to look closely,' she added, 'because of the smell.'

Without interrupting her story, she crossed her arms in a Chinese gesture of obeisance, seized the shoulders of her dress and began to pull it over her head. Ozzie placidly regarded a pair of plump thighs, constrained within stahlex knitted stockings; and a moment later a diminutive pair of panties, emblazoned with a frank invitation in polished stahlex diamante.

'It wasn't until the dog started to run that I saw its back legs were funny.' The dress, owing to its tightness, became stuck somewhere under her armpits. Her voice issued through its muffling folds. 'So the dog dragged itself round and round in a circle, with this maniac lashing at it, and me standing in the middle like a circus clown or something.'

Ozzie didn't want to watch and he didn't want to listen. It all had to do with a world he didn't want to believe in.

'There was another funny thing,' she said in a strangled voice, but then managed to pull the dress over her head and spoke with a sudden clarity. 'The dog was called "Dad".'

'Funny,' he agreed.

Tentrix twisted on one foot, and then on the other. She smiled at him, crooked her index finger three times in a summons to follow her, and made for the connecting door.

'No!' He took a pace forwards.

She stopped at the door and looked at him over her bare shoulder. 'It's the sleeping-cubicle, isn't it? You don't expect me to lie on the floor?'

'Please don't go in there!' He stretched his arms towards her.

Her blue eyes questioned him. He stood rigidly, helplessly, his arms outstretched. With a snort of laughter she pushed open the door and went through into the other cubicle.

'No!'

He stumbled after her. The shock of seeing Tentrix in the middle of that dear and familiar scene made him tremble.

Half the available space was occupied by the bed, which for some weeks had been permanently unfolded from the wall. The remaining floor area was covered by the faded quilt on which they were standing, and a soiled pillow. He had taken to sleeping on the floor soon after the beginning of his quest.

But it was the bed which held Tentrix's attention.

'What's all this?'

The bed was dressed with a spotless white sheet, immaculately draped and without creases. On the sheet his treasures were meticulously arranged in an orderly series, floor by floor and vestibule by vestibule. Each item had a neatly printed label.

'It's my collection,' he said.

'But what *are* they?'

He realized that she didn't really know what they were, seeing so many of them in one place, and out of their usual context. To him, also, the actual name for them was strangely inadequate, and somehow detracted from what they really were.

'What are they?' she demanded.

'Door handles.'

'Door . . . But how did they get to be here?'

Ozzie didn't want to talk to her. He wanted her to put on her clothes and go away.

'I collect them.'

She swivelled her eyes to his face. 'Why?'

He knew he couldn't explain to her. He would never be able to explain to anybody.

'Why?' she insisted.

'It's because they sort of . . . sort of suggest that there might be a pattern in things.'

Tentrix's expression of disbelief began to change into one of amusement. Her small mouth widened, and her lips opened to show the small white teeth. She returned her attention to the bed, and picked up a handle in the shape of a small ring.

'Please put it down,' he asked, desperately.

She read from the label, choking with amusement.

'Vestibule 333, off corridor 18, floor 87. This was the beginning although I did not know it at the time.'

Laughter overwhelmed her. She collapsed on the bed and rolled over on to her back. Tears of merriment sparkled in her eyes. The door handles jangled together on the crumpled sheet, and tinkled an accompaniment to her hilarity. The ring from vestibule 333 escaped from her hand and came to rest at Ozzie's feet.

Tentrix put her hand to her aching stomach, too exhausted to laugh any more. She lay with her mouth open, tears of mirth at the corners of her eyes, gasping for breath.

He bent down, picked up the ring, and popped it into the moist cavity. Her eyes opened wide, then terribly wide, as he pressed with his fingers until the ring was a snug fit behind her small teeth. Her tongue came out through the hole, swollen and blue. The ring seemed to be turning, spinning like a wheel.

The door handles started to jangle again, in a frantic accompaniment to her drumming heels. They didn't stop their tintinnabulation until her heels came to rest.

CHAPTER THIRTY-ONE

As soon as Jan Caspol entered the West Gatehouse he could see that Sylvia was distressed.

Dixon came forward. 'What would you like to drink, sir?'

Jan looked at her. She made no motion, but her eyes thanked him for returning on time and told him that she wanted to go.

'Nothing, thank you Dixon. It's quite late and I think we'll get back and rescue Sperry from his nursery.'

'Very good, sir. Thank you, sir.'

They came out into the night air and were walking towards the autopark.

'Thank you, Jan.'

He stopped and kissed her on the mouth. 'What's the matter?'

She turned away and continued towards the auto. The doors opened and closed noiselessly behind them, and he reset the co-ordinates for Lindisfarne. The parking struts retracted, and the soundless turbines swept them away. The wide, low beams of the headlights turned night into day on the northbound autoway.

Sylvia lay back with her hands clasped behind her head and looked up through the transparent roof at the night sky. He turned to look at her. Starlight glittered momentarily on the circle of the Celtic cross she wore round her neck.

'Haven't you had an interesting day?' he asked.

'Yes.'

'That's good, then.'

'It was interesting in the sense that I discovered a number of things I hadn't expected. Horrible things.'

'I'm sorry.'

He reached for her hand, but she removed it.

On their right the red deer looked up and blinked in the temporary daylight. Farther away, beyond the reach of the passing beam, the coniferous forest almost totally concealed the colossal automated factories of the Stahlex Corporation. Only the fractionating tower rose above the tallest firs, and its spangled height added an artificial constellation to the sky.

'Why not tell me about it?' he suggested.

She continued to stare upwards through the transparent roof. 'The first man I met was motivated by a desire to make profits, and the second——'

Jan's hoot of laughter interrupted her. 'Did he wear a bowler hat and a waistcoat with the bottom button undone?

And did he have a briefcase with a gilt monogram on the flap?'

'You have identified the type,' she agreed, without amusement, 'although he was without those external stigmata.'

He snapped his fingers, in the ritual gesture used by old movie-makers to indicate that a man had just made a decision. 'I shall throw away my economic history books,' he announced, 'and study things at first-hand in Tcity.'

'The second man,' she continued, 'had suffered a traumatic experience in his boyhood.'

'What was it?'

'I didn't find out. But it must have been pretty dreadful. His only motive for working was to escape from his memories for a few hours every day.'

Sylvia continued to stare upwards through the transparent roof. They were cocooned in silence as the auto sped through open country to the northern limb of Tcity.

He prompted her. 'I thought you were going to see four people?'

'The third man was a simple case. He worked so as to have more money to buy more pleasure. He'll get more aphrodollies and more auto rides that way.'

'I guess that was always a common type.'

'The fourth man was the most interesting, I think. He had some kind of obsession.'

'What was it?'

'He wouldn't tell me. But it obviously made him happy.'

'Obsessed people are happy people in their own way,' he said. 'They don't need the consolations of religion or philosophy. That shows your Work Project is a success.'

She contradicted him in a low voice. 'That's just the point. The fourth man had just decided to leave his job.'

'Sylvia, after listening to your experiences, I can't really understand why you should be so disappointed.'

She turned her head sideways on her linked hands and looked at him. 'You *can't*! You *really* can't!' Her head rolled back and she continued to look up through the transparent roof. 'When I reflect that it was I who introduced the Work Project into Tcity, and when I think about the four empty lives of those four empty men . . .'

Sylvia drew a rapid breath and screamed. 'Jan! Jan! Where are the stars?'

He quickly seized her shoulders, and turned her to face him. 'What's the matter with you? We're in the tunnel.'

In front of them the headlights had come on, illuminating the bore of the tunnel under the Sixth Sector. The hiss of the reinforced tyres was faintly audible as the sound bounced back from the walls.

She half-laughed, half-sobbed. 'I'm sorry. Today's experiences have disappointed me.'

'Why?' He spoke gently but firmly. 'The Work Project has benefited all the people you saw. The first man has a motive for living which he would otherwise be without. The second is better able to forget his unhappy memories. The third can more easily gratify his ordinary human desires. And the fourth man, for all we know, learned to enjoy his obsession the more keenly because he was unable to indulge it during working hours. But even if you've improved the lot of only three of them, your sample shows a success rate of seventy-five per cent for the Work Project.'

'But think of their lives!' she complained. 'Think of their lives, Jan!'

He put his arm round her shoulders. 'Men have different faces. There are no two alike, and you can't expect them to wear the same mask.' He grinned. 'Even Buddhas only point the way.'

'I'm sorry,' she said. 'I should have asked you about your day. Did you like Arthur Medway?'

The auto continued to flee through the darkness. Jan recalled the elderly monk, cracking nuts and extracting the kernels with quiet pleasure; the firm assurance of the handshake and the inward smile; the final slow wave of farewell from the shadows of the gateway.

'He was a very good man. I shall never forget him.'

The auto fled from the tunnel and followed the coast road with the straight flight of a fulmar. The hiss of the tyres was reabsorbed by the night air and they travelled in silence.

She smiled. 'You're not thinking of assuming the saffron robe, are you?'

'No. Life is too sweet.'

The stars had reappeared. Their light was reflected on the ring in the Celtic cross at Sylvia's throat; and the same light sparkled on the crests of the North Sea waves as they rolled on to the silver sands and expired, to be followed by the crests of newborn waves in their wake, which expired and were replaced in turn by those that followed.

PROTECTOR

Larry Niven

Phssthpok the Pak had been travelling for most of his 32,000 years – his mission, to save, develop and protect the group of pak breeders sent out into space some 2½ million years before . . .

Brennan was a Belter, the product of a fiercely independent, somewhat anarchic society living in, on and around an outer asteroid belt. The Belters were rebels one and all, and Brennan was a Smuggler. The Belt worlds had been tracking the pak ship for days – Brennan figured to meet that ship first . . .

He was never seen again – at least not in the form of homo sapiens.

Larry Niven is the author of RINGWORLD which won both the Hugo and Nebula awards for the best s.f. novel of the year.

THE FLIGHT OF THE HORSE

Larry Niven

These are the stories of Svetz the harassed Time Retrieval Expert and of the mind-bending difficulties created when his Department supplies him with inadequate information . . .

Here too are his strange adventures with horses, unicorns, ostriches, rocs and other unlikely fauna, both extinct and as yet unborn . . . In THE FLIGHT OF THE HORSE, Larry Niven has written a collection of science fiction stories which combine fantasy and mainstream s.f. with superb story telling.

THE FOREVER WAR

Joe Haldeman

Winner of the 1976 Nebula and Hugo Awards.

Earth has been fighting for its life against an alien civilization which simply will not negotiate.

The elite of Earth's young people are trained to fight a war fought at speeds approaching that of light. Relativity comes into play. A group of young people will leave the Earth aged 27 and return *two of their years later* to find that the Earth and war have moved on by fifty, a hundred, maybe several hundred years.

Making brilliant use of this paradox and the well nigh impossible logistics of fighting such a war, Joe Haldeman has given us the most impressive SF novel of the past ten years – an instant classic.

THE MOTE IN GOD'S EYE

Larry Niven and Jerry Pournelle

An alien space ship, using some motive power unknown to man, comes sailing into the outer reaches of the solar system.

The team sent to intercept it accidentally destroy it, but its course has been recorded accurately enough to extrapolate its point of origin.

A team of scientists, escorted by the most powerful battleship in Earth's space fleet is sent to contact this newly discovered civilization. What they find is at once the most exciting and tragic destiny ever to be suffered by sentient beings.

'The best novel about human beings making first contact with intelligent but utterly nonhuman aliens I have ever seen, and possibly the finest science fiction novel I have ever read.'
Robert A. Heinlein.

'A spellbinder, a swashbuckler . . . and best of all a brilliant new approach to that fascinating problem – first contact with aliens.'
Frank Herbert

FUTURA CASH SALES,
110 WARNER ROAD,
LONDON SE5

Please send me the following titles

Quantity	SBN	Title	Amount
______			______
______			______
______			______
______			______
______			______
			______
		TOTAL	______

Please enclose a cheque or postal order made out to FUTURA PUBLICATIONS LIMITED for the amount due, including 10p per book to allow for postage and packing. Orders will take about three weeks to reach you and we cannot accept responsibility for orders containing cash.

PLEASE PRINT CLEARLY

NAME...

ADDRESS ....

....

....